THE BLACK PLAGUE

Billy Pepitone

Disclaimer:

This is a work of fiction. Names, characters, businesses, places, events, locales, and incident are either the product of the author's imagination or used in a fictitious manner. Any resemblance to actual persons, living or dead, or actual events is purely coincidental.

ISBN # 9798842898138

U.S. Library of Congress 1-11522661871

2022

Dedicated to those we lost and continue to lose, for all the wrong reasons.

"Blind faith in your leaders, or in anything, will get you killed."

-Bruce Springsteen

1

"A city mortally wounded by its own hand, slowly fading into a tragic, violent abyss."

-BlueWave.com

AUGUST 2022

Heat. Humidity. Fear.

All were palpable as the full moon offered the only light on West 56th Street and Hull Avenue, the burned-out streetlights in various stages of disrepair for several months. A tall, broad shouldered young man stood next to the graffiti-covered mailbox and overfilled trash can, his head pivoting back and forth as he waited for a man he knew only as Phil to deliver him an envelope of cash. That cash would go directly to his boss, and every dollar had to be accounted for. One dollar short would cost him a finger. Any more could cost him his life.

As midnight approached, a strong summer wind pushed down the avenue, swirling papers and discarded bottles near the man's feet. He looked at his wrist to check the time, cursing his stupidity as he realized he had left his watch on his dresser back at his dilapidated studio apartment on the East Side. A car would pass every few minutes, the headlights blinding as they reflected off vacant store windows. The once bustling strip had been devastated over the past two years, a thriving economic artery severed and reduced to near apocalyptic conditions. The police were not a concern as they avoided the area, citing manpower issues. The perfect setting for the illicit transfer of funds.

His business, the only line of work he had ever known in his nineteen years on earth, was still quite viable, however. Of course, those he reported to reaped most of the rewards, he himself settling for crumbs and a purpose in life, no matter how sordid. His previous assignment was far more complicated and high profile, the results exactly what had been promised, except there had been recent complications regarding the physical well-being of his cohorts. Still, all he had to do right now was collect the envelope from Phil and bring it directly to his boss. No stops, no phone calls, no excuses. A simple existence for a simple young man.

"Hi Bernard."

The man looked around, wondering whose voice he had heard, and how they knew his name. He knew it couldn't be Phil, as his contact had never spoken a single word to him during any of their previous encounters. There was no one around, except for the stray, black and white dog hobbling across the street. The man shook his head and blamed it on the wind and his imagination, silently praying that it wasn't…

"Waiting for someone?"

Again, the man checked around him, finding no one. This time he was sure he was not imagining things, as the voice sounded closer and clearer. His heart rate increasing, he began walking up 56th Street, away from the drop point, an inexcusable sin in his boss' eyes.

"Going somewhere, Bernard?"

"Who's there?" the man shouted, his voice cracking as it echoed down the desolate, dimly lit street. "Who the hell are you?"

A large-framed figure stepped out from behind an old, abandoned postal truck, the man unable to see a face in the darkness. As the shape drew closer, Bernard Williams felt its two flaming red eyes lock onto and burn through his heart.

"Jesus Christ, it's you!" Bernard screamed as he ran up the street toward Mikita Avenue. His searing heart pounding through his chest, he looked over his shoulder to see if he was being pursued. The shape was gone, but not the unmistakable sense of dread. As he was about to turn left on Mikita, the black monster with the fire burning in its eyes dropped out of nowhere in front of him.

"It's your turn, Bernard."

"Listen," the man said, his body trembling in fear. "I didn't do anything. I swear!"

"You killed Anna Winston. You and your friends. They've met their maker. Now it's your turn."

"No, I swear," the man cried as he back peddled up the street, the monster slowly hunting its prey. "It wasn't us. You don't understand-"

"Liar!"

"Please, you don't understand," the man pled as he tripped and fell backwards onto the sidewalk. "We didn't kill anyone. It wasn't us. I swear to God!"

"You can swear all you want to him, in person."

The man felt a vice-like grip on his lower right arm, an intense pain shooting up to his shoulder. There was a snap and a blood curdling cry as he crumpled to the ground, his forearm ulna bone protruding through his skin.

"No! Please, don't kill me!" the man begged as he rolled on the sidewalk in agony, the sight of the compound fracture making him sick to his stomach.

"Anna Winston pleaded for her life, too. You didn't care then. I don't care now."

"I swear, we didn't-"

The monster unleashed several blows to the man's face, crushing his orbital bones. He then latched onto the man's chin and forehead and, in one violent motion, snapped his neck from left to right, severing his spinal cord. The man slumped to the ground, heavy and lifeless.

The summer wind picked up again as the man lie in a pool of his own blood, the dark figure sliding undetected back into the night as quickly as he appeared. The violence sewed itself into the sultry heat, whistling across the deteriorating landscape of a city near death.

###

Lieutenant Clayton Morgan removed his foggy eyeglasses and looked down at the bloody, mangled body lying on the steamy asphalt and shook his head. He knew immediately who the victim was, though the facial injuries hideously altered the appearance. It was number four, which Morgan anticipated, though no one else in the apathetic city seemed to care.

Morgan walked away as an ambulance pulled up to the scene, the paramedics making their way past several cops who seemed uninterested in the body at their feet. His detectives would be arriving momentarily, taking photos and searching for witnesses along with any sliver of evidence, of which he was sure they would find none. During his previous twenty-nine years on the Harbor City Police Department, he had never come across a crime scene where there wasn't at least a shred of something useful. Someone who may have heard or seen something, surveillance camera footage from nearby establishments, a single hair or drop of dried blood. There was always something. That all changed two weeks earlier. With his thirtieth work anniversary looming in less than twenty days,

Morgan now had three career criminals lying in the morgue, and a fourth soon to be joining them. There was only one connection; one that provided far too many obstacles to overcome.

"Let me guess," a voice called out from behind the yellow and black crime scene tape wrapped around the unlit light pole at the corner of West 56th Street. "Karma caught up to the last member of the Fab Four."

Morgan scowled as he looked over at the familiar face, that of his former subordinate and verbal sparring mate for over ten years. "It's three in the morning. Shouldn't you be crawling out of a bar with a ten dollar hooker around this time?"

"Did that about two hours ago," replied Keith Lincoln, a disheveled looking man, dressed in his normal late night carousing ensemble of baggy blue jeans, dirty white sneakers and a rumpled, oversized navy blue sports jacket. "And she cost me twenty."

"Post-pandemic inflation," Morgan said as he walked over, studying the scene from the corner. "Well, if nothing else, this gives you more shit to write about on that stupid blob of yours."

"It's called a blog, and that stupid blog of mine is the most popular website in the city, I'll have you know," Lincoln said, his words slightly slurred. "Thanks to my anonymous source, of course."

"Your anonymous source will have his ass hung from the flag pole at City Hall if they find out who it is," Morgan said as he took a step back from the inebriated man. "Dammit, Skippy, what the hell did you drink tonight? You stink like cheap after-shave and onions."

"Whiskey, my friend. Straight whiskey. Oh, with some fried Kielbasa. Not easy finding Polish hookers who can cook. Got lucky tonight, I guess."

Morgan shook his head as he waved his arms to chase the odor away. "When was the last time you showered, Skippy?"

Lincoln thought for a moment. "What month is this?"

"Jesus, you're a train wreck," Morgan said as two detectives from his squad arrived on the scene. "But I've got bigger problems than your overwhelmingly bad hygiene. I've got some crazy bastard running around at night kicking the living shit out of people. You know who doesn't need this aggravation right now?"

"I'm guessing here, but…you?" Lincoln replied.

"Damn straight, Skippy," Morgan snapped. "Thirty goddam years and now I gotta get called on the carpet for this crap?"

"I hate when you call me Skippy, for the record," Lincoln said. "But why are you worried? We both know this is Bernard Williams. We've been expecting this."

"That doesn't make me feel any better," Morgan said as flashing lights illuminated the street. "Our only suspect is the old man, but no one's gonna let me bring Charlie Winston in for questioning. Too many powerful allies and famous lawyers with deep pockets. They'll boot my skinny ass to traffic cop."

"Well I'm pretty sure Bernard's not gonna be able to give you much. What about those?"

Morgan looked up toward the surveillance camera posted high above the light pole on the opposite corner. "Mayor's office shut down all the city surveillance cameras last year. People complaining about Big Brother watching. Bunch of bullshit. Don't you watch the news?"

"Right, I forgot," Lincoln replied. "Oh well. Maybe you'll get lucky and a witness-"

"Yeah, sure," Morgan interjected angrily. "No one sees anything in this city anymore, and if they do, they ain't talkin."

"Maybe there's nothing to see?"

"What the hell are you talkin' about, fool?" Morgan shouted. "You think the Invisible Man is beating these stink bug, dirt bags to death?"

Lincoln yawned, the lieutenants' simmering frustration level not uncommon. "The old man has the money to make people forget what they've seen, that's all I'm saying. You need to talk to him, no matter what the brass says."

"You don't think I know that, Skippy? I went straight to Belanger, and she cut me down to my skivvies."

"So the Police Commissioner is running interference in a multiple homicide investigation? Interesting."

"You put that on your blob and the mayor and commissioner will shit ice cubes in August," Morgan snapped. "Let's just stick with hoodlums on hoodlums. Stink bugs killin' stink bugs. No one cares about four ex-cons, so let's leave it that way."

"Hoodlums, or stink bugs as you say, ain't gonna help me get more page views and users, you know. No views equals no advertisers, which equals no money. Hitmen hired by vengeful zillionaires, now that grabs attention. So do vigilantes, comprende?"

"Don't even go there, Skippy."

Lincoln studied the uniformed cops standing near the body, surprised that one in particular was not present. "Where's Wilson? This is his sector, isn't it?"

"Muscle Head called out sick tonight," Morgan growled. "Probably got some fake tan spray in his eyes again."

Lincoln let out a loud, elongated belch. "Probably. Anyway, can you just give me one quote from an anonymous source for this? I'll take anything."

"Okay. How about this. Keith Lincoln, former hot shit detective, is a goddam mess and needs to change his socks and wash his ass," Morgan said as he headed back toward the ambulance. "This time try and spell anonymous right, okay?"

"That's not helpful at all!" Lincoln shouted before slinking away into the darkness, where he took several pictures of the crime scene on his cell phone as Morgan met with his detectives and the battered body was removed to Harbor City Hospital on the East Side. He quickly headed home to his rent-controlled apartment on West 11th Street off of Kingman

Avenue. Uneven on his feet, he walked past an unconscious homeless man he had come to know simply as Ralph, lying on the buildings' front steps. He gingerly climbed over the man and took the rickety elevator to the sixth floor where he opened the door to Apartment 6B. Inside his refrigerator sat a half-full bottle of orange juice and several slices of yellow American cheese, which would have to suffice as breakfast.

Lincoln rubbed his bleary eyes and stretched out his aching body as he sat in front of his desktop computer. It had been yet another long night, and sleep had all but abandoned him at this stage of his life. Too many bad memories, too many regrets, both distant and recent. The screen lit up, the words BLUEWAVE.COM appearing in bold lettering. He tapped at the keyboard quickly and relentlessly, the story a bit disjointed as he still had very little to go on since Morgan appeared to be getting cold feet when it came to supplying real time information.

At approximately two thirty this morning Western District cops found an unidentified male on Fifty Sixth Street near Mikita. Though the victim hasn't been ID'd yet, it's pretty obvious the fourth domino has fallen. Bernard Williams, the last remaining parolee who walked free after committing the most high-profile crime in the city's history. No matter what the District Attorney ruled, you and I both know it was a set-up, and we're all paying the price.

The job won't come out and say it, but does anyone doubt the old man has had a hand in all of this? But cops can't get near him, so we're left with breadcrumb bullshit about rival street gangs or random assaults.

Maybe I'm wrong about all of this. Maybe it's not the old man. Maybe Harbor City has a real-life vigilante who has seen enough. An ordinary, pissed off citizen who reached their breaking point after the pandemic lockdowns that drove us all a bit insane and broke this city. Someone who lost their job, their livelihood, or maybe a family member who they weren't able to visit in the hospital because of the ridiculous mandates. Maybe they finally snapped? Do we applaud them? Lock them up? Key to the city? Time will tell, ladies and gentlemen. The brass can't keep this quiet much longer. Just know, I'm watching, as usual.

Goodnight from the shadows.

-Bluewave.com

2

Four months earlier…

The sun once again rose over Harbor City, Illinois, despite constant predictions to the contrary. Charles Winston looked out across the April morning and memories, both glorious and frightening, flooded his mind. Once an economic powerhouse just ninety miles west of Chicago, the thriving metropolis had been devastated by the Coronavirus pandemic of 2020. The virus, having originated out of China by still unconfirmed and controversial means, affected over five hundred thousand of the city's two million residents, causing nearly six thousand deaths. Nationally, over nine hundred thousand Americans died from Coronavirus-related symptoms. The fear that rippled throughout Harbor City during the first few weeks of the outbreak turned into a full-blown wave of hysteria as casualties and deaths piled up, while local media outlets sensationalized the panic. Mayor Martin 'Marty' McSorley expedited the decline with two disastrous decisions that acted as gut punches that put Harbor City down for the count; implementing lockdowns that kept residents bottled up in their homes for three weeks, and the release of prisoners from William J. Carothers Prison in an ill-fated attempt to try and stem the flow of the virus within the prison walls. Small businesses disappeared and livelihoods were destroyed, while nearly two hundred 'non-violent' offenders were released into society unchecked. While the majority assimilated peacefully back into everyday life, there were those who were unable or unwilling. They took the mayor's pardon not as a sign of mercy but of weakness and decided to take what they felt was owed to them for their incarceration. The crime rate, which had been relatively low in comparison to other major cities, suddenly skyrocketed as the city quickly fell into despair. The streets were no longer safe as a dystopian atmosphere settled in with little resistance from those charged with doing such.

The most controversial decision by the McSorley administration was to mandate Coronavirus vaccinations for every citizen and essential worker. Those who did not comply were no longer eligible to work or were terminated from their employment. McSorley lobbied hard for residents and employees to take a vaccination produced by Oliver Industries, a major Northeast-based pharmaceutical company, rather than three other vaccinations approved by the Center for Disease

Control. His over-the-top promotion of Oliver's product raised many eyebrows, though suspicions eventually faded as shouts of protest went unheard.

Two years had passed since the failed lockdown had been lifted, and Harbor City was a shell of its former self. The streets were still a hazard to navigate; robberies, assaults and rapes were up over fifty-five percent from pre-pandemic days in early 2020. Homicides were up thirty percent, and shootings nearly seventy percent. Those who had been released by McSorley had formed roving street gangs loyal to the city's most powerful organized crime family and benefitted from the flow of weapons and political influence. The Harbor City Police Department, demoralized by the deaths of ten officers who contracted the virus and a city whose crumbling economy could not afford to better protect its members, had taken a hands-off policy toward crime, resorting to ineffective, reactive policing that reduced the police to after-the-fact report takers. Morale had been destroyed, and there were no signs of revival.

The most devastating and publicized crime that took place during the pandemic was the horrific murder of Anna Winston, a fifty-seven-year-old socialite married to Harbor City's wealthiest financier, the seventy-year-old billionaire who held the title of the sixth richest man in the world. On March

19th, 2021, on an unseasonably warm afternoon, and with Charles away on business in France and unable to return due to flight restrictions caused by the spreading virus, Mrs. Winston decided to leave her Harbor view apartment and take a stroll on the pier. Having become stir crazy from being alone and isolated in her penthouse, the stunning blonde felt the fresh air would calm her mind. For several minutes, it had succeeded, until something heinous occurred. The woman's body was found in a grass field less than a quarter mile from the pier. She had been beaten and suffered severe head trauma, which was ruled the cause of her death. Only her six-thousand-dollar Cartier watch had been taken from her body. A homeless man interviewed by police informed them he had witnessed four young men in their late teens or early twenties talking with the socialite. Just hours later, an astute homicide detective found four men fitting the description walking in an area near the crime scene. He stopped them, and when their stories didn't corroborate, they were brought in for questioning. At that point, the watch was recovered from one of the men's coats. The suspects, each of whom were recent benefactors of early prison release, blamed one another and were arrested and charged with murder.

Anna Winston was pronounced dead at the scene, as a distraught Charles used every ounce of his politically connected muscle to charter a private flight home.

The funeral, which would normally have brought hundreds of the wealthiest and most powerful in the country together to mourn, was instead a private affair consisting of only Charles and Monsignor Roger Sarno from nearby St. Monica's Church. Douglas Detwiler, Illinois' first term Governor who was struggling to keep the state's second most famous city afloat, sent his condolences along with those of Police Commissioner Kathleen Belanger. Mayor McSorley stayed away and avoided the anticipated media onslaught as well as Charles Winston's ire.

The city heard all about Charles' descent into a deep depression, his self-imposed exile a regular news item each night. Each morning after the funeral, he watched the sun rise over the harbor from his living room window, peering out at the famous Harbor City Lighthouse. He thought of his wife and all that he had lost that fateful day. The small fortune he had lost as the city and nation's economy crumbled meant nothing to him compared to his wife's brutal death. He told himself he missed her dearly, and swore he saw her face high up in the clouds each morning, her smile assuring her husband his life could still go on, if he would just pick himself up and move past everything that had happened.

Several months later, the judicial system would add to the pain caused by the horrendous crime, as the case against the four defendants was dropped in a controversial decision that shook the city to its core and only exacerbated the lack of faith in local government.

On the one-year anniversary of Anna's murder, local news outlets ran lead stories about the angry and bitter billionaire. They peeled back the curtain and exposed a lost and lonely man. Charles Winston emerged from exile for a brief period, holding a press conference to assure his wealthy clients that he was indeed very much alive, and it was business as usual. He explained how he had thrown himself into religion, studying Christian, Hebrew and Muslim faith. While it did little to extinguish the fire burning deep inside him, it did offer him a direction to channel his rage. His jittery clients were still nervous, but glad to see their golden goose back in the public eye even for the briefest of periods.

What they didn't know was that he had formulated a plan in his mind, fending off his conscience during their daily battles. The plan was obscene, unreasonable, and unworthy of discussing with anyone other than his most loyal servant. Yet he salivated at the thought of pulling it off. Not only would it save his city, but it would also feed the beast of revenge gnawing at the heart of every law-abiding citizen.

His chauffeur and executive aide, a towering, muscular man named Ernest Lenning, opened the door to the office and led a younger man inside. He pulled out the chair across from where Winston sat and motioned for the man to sit. The man slowly complied, looking around the spacious office with confusion. The billionaire studied the man's bewildered expression, something he obviously anticipated.

"You're confused, but curious," Winston said in his normal soft, reserved tone of voice. "You want to know why you're here, correct?"

The man nodded, looking over his shoulder at Ernest who stood near the antique bookcase in the southeast corner of the room. "Look, we've been over your wife's case a thousand times, Mr. Winston. I've apologized to you another thousand for how everything turned out. What else is there to talk about?"

Winston smiled. "Quite a lot. Quite a lot indeed."

The man leaned back in his chair and crossed his arms. "Mr. Winston, I've gotta lot to do today. Can we cut to the chase?"

"Why, certainly," Winston replied, appreciating the man's desire for bluntness. "This city was my life, still is in many ways. I worked my way up from local shelf stocker at McMahon's Grocery on Eighth to this penthouse. My wife and I met here, courted, and later married. Every wonderful memory I have of her is framed by Harbor City. But this city, rather the cowards that ran it to the ground, took her away from me, and took my memories with it. I can't bring my Anna back, but I can bring my city back by punishing those who destroyed my life."

The man, cynic by nature and circumstance, looked sideways at the billionaire. "Ok, and how do you plan on doing this, exactly? You want revenge, I'm guessing. So you go after those four who killed Anna, and then you gotta kill McSorley, who's got four or five detectives on his security detail, and the District Attorney who tanked the whole damn case. That's a high body count."

"McSorley's day will come, I promise you that," Winston said with conviction. "The same for District Attorney

Flagg. But for now, they are not my priority. Those he freed, those who preyed on innocents like my Anna, they must be dealt with first."

"I'm gathering you don't have much faith in the cops taking care of this."

Winston sighed and raised his right eyebrow.

"Yeah, scratch that," the man said with a laugh, amused by his own words. "Okay, so next question. Why me, and what the hell can I do about anything? Haven't I screwed up enough?"

"Yes, you have," Winston replied with a smirk, straightening in his chair. "Therefore, the way I see it, you owe me."

"Owe you?" the man said with an even louder laugh. "Look, you know how sorry I am about what happened to Anna, but I got screwed over big time by McSorley and Flagg, got my name dragged through the gutter and lost my job over this case. Lost my marriage. I'd say somebody owes me something."

"Very well, then. I believe we are in a unique position where we can help each other immensely."

The man shook his head, unconvinced and skeptical. "I don't see how."

"I have the resources, or can acquire those I don't," Winston said. "All I need to begin is your trust and your loyalty."

The man looked straight into the billionaires' steely gaze and realized he was serious. "Okay, I'll play along for now. What's your big secret plan?"

"Oh, I believe you'll approve," Winston said with a glimmer of satisfaction. "Tell me, have you ever studied scripture?"

3

Keisha Hamilton finished her ten-hour shift at the Harborview Diner, grabbed her pocketbook and headed out the door into the humid night. It was shortly past midnight, her feet aching as she began the eight block walk back to her apartment on Payton Street. Reaching into her pocket she fiddled with the eighteen dollars in tips she had made that night, a far cry from what she was earning in the diner's pre-pandemic days. On nights like these she wondered if going to work at all was worth it, but each time she reminded herself of her two-year-old son Brian, conceived during the city lockdown. Brian's father left soon after Keisha had informed him of her pregnancy, the two-month fling costing her dearly but bringing a new light into her dark world.

The streets were busy, filled with those who could no longer afford the once taken-for- granted luxuries of air conditioning. Midnight looked the same as noon, except for the bright, full moon that hovered above the lingering, lost souls. Keisha dodged the catcalls and tin cans of those begging for money, a nightly, post-shift ritual for her. She was no longer afraid, instead focusing her mind on her little boy and the peaceful sleep he would be in under the watchful eye of his grandmother.

Upon reaching the corner of Bannerman Avenue and Ninth Street, she heard an unnerving sound coming from behind. Heavy footsteps, unlike any she had heard during her nightly walks home. She quickened her pace, trying to stay ahead of whomever it was. But the footsteps stayed in stride, gaining ground, closing in.

As she reached the middle of the block, she could almost feel the hot breath on the back of her neck. She tried to run, but her legs did not respond to her brain's message. She spun around to face her pursuer while reaching into her purse, desperately searching for the can of pepper spray her mother had bought her two weeks earlier. As she fumbled with the contents of her purse, she was grabbed by her throat and dragged into the side alley next to the deserted electronics store.

Keisha struggled in the man's powerful grip, her attempt to escape futile. He was a hulking figure, over six feet tall and close to three hundred pounds. His salt and pepper beard rubbed roughly against her face, his lifeless, black eyes looking right through hers. She felt her life slipping away, her prayers going unanswered as her mind shifted to Brian, and how he was going to grow up without her in this mean, violent world she had brought him into.

The man reached under her skirt, ripping her panties down as she started losing consciousness. His face was blurred, his awful scent fading away as her eyes began to close. Then, for some reason, he stopped. He dropped the helpless woman to the grimy alley floor, looking into the darkness toward the rear of the building. He took a step forward before calling out, his voice bellowing and echoing seemingly across the entire city.

"Who the hell is back there?" he shouted. There was no answer, just the cries of scattering stray cats frightened by whatever they had just encountered in the dark. He reached into his pocket with his left hand and drew a six-inch folding knife as he walked slowly down the alley. "I will gut you, you sunavabitch. Come out here so I can see you, bitch."

Keisha raised her head off the ground, her vision still blurry and her head spinning. She saw the back of her attacker drifting away, the outline of the knife in his hand. She heard him call out into the darkness again, challenging whomever he thought was there to face him. Her attacker's massive body suddenly disappeared. She heard the screams, the horrific wails.

After a few seconds, the cries stopped. Keisha lowered her head to the pavement and passed out.

###

The Lakeside Tavern had all but emptied out as the clock struck four a.m., the bar lights dimmed by sixty-year-old Sammy Jones, the owner, bartender, and King of all Harbor City gossip. Jones, who had run the business for over thirty years, had lived through the city's glory days and its recent descent. He knew every cop on the beat by name, many of whom were steady customers. The one patron left in the back of the bar was an old friend who started closing the place down with him almost every night for the past three months.

"Last one's on me," Jones said as he placed a beer down on the table in front of Keith Lincoln. "Rough night, kid?"

"They're all rough, Sammy," Lincoln said as he eyed the glass. "Life's not getting any easier."

"Saw you talking to Sergeant Flaherty before. Looked like you were in deep conversation."

"Another guy got his ass whipped a few hours ago, down on Bannerman behind Eddie's Electronics," Lincoln said. "The brass are doing quite a job keeping this one under wraps. Nothing on social media anywhere."

"I'm surprised you haven't blown the lid off this thing yet," Jones said, pushing the beer closer to the suddenly reluctant man. "Morgan stop giving you info?"

"The boss is afraid they might figure out he's the leak and launch him into retirement," Lincoln said. "If they only knew half the job talks to me."

"And the other half hates you." Jones laughed, only partially kidding.

Lincoln lifted the glass to his lips but was quickly distracted by Clayton Morgan entering through the back door. "Well, well. Speak of the devil," Lincoln said. "Pull up a chair, boss. Heard our friend dropped another one for you guys."

"Yeah, but he let this one live, barely," The weary looking lieutenant sat down at the table as Sammy headed back to the bar to fetch another beer. "This is bat shit crazy, like out of a low-rent, B-rated horror flick. Somebody tell me this is all a goddam joke?"

"Wish I could," Lincoln said, leaning toward the lieutenant. "I hope you got more info for me than Flaherty had."

"Listen here, Skippy," an exasperated, exhausted Morgan snapped. "Flaherty's a big mouth, fish-face lookin' fool who doesn't know his ass from his elbow. Don't be printing nothing that dope says."

"Okay, okay," Lincoln held his hands up in mock surrender. "I won't. I'm sorry. I'm all ears."

"Waitress walking home after work, down near Ninth. Big guy follows her, drags her into an alley behind the electronics store. Starts to rape her but stops. Walks down the alley, ends up with a broken arm, broken leg and probably a broken skull. Got half his teeth knocked down his throat. Somebody messed his shit up bad."

"And?" Lincoln asked for more as Sammy rejoined the duo at the table.

"No one saw a goddam thing. I just interviewed the victim at the hospital. She blacked out, doesn't remember much."

"Anything on our wanna-be rapist?" Lincoln asked.

"Benny Barnes."

Lincoln was surprised. "Barnes? He has no connection to the Winston case."

"Dunno yet," Morgan said, shaking his head. "He's got some ties to Bernard Williams, ran in the same circles, but wasn't implicated in the Winston murder. So it begs the question..."

"Why let this one live?"

"I say the dirtbag deserved what he got," Sammy interjected as he raised his own glass. "When you find this guy, tell him he's welcome here anytime. Everything's on the house."

"I don't need this shit right now," Morgan said as he chugged his beer. "Me and the wife are going to Miami next month and I'm gonna spend every day at the goddam beach. I don't give a flyin' rat's ass who's running around at night taking these guys out. Not gonna be my problem for six beautiful, sunny days."

"You and your wife?" Lincoln asked, surprise in his voice. "You've been divorced from Michelle for five years, boss."

"So we had a little argument. No big deal."

"She ran off with your dog walker." Lincoln reminded him.

"What?" Morgan shouted. "We had a dog?"

"Never mind." Lincoln sighed.

"Unless you've got some answers for me I suggest you shut your pie hole, Skippy," Morgan snarled.

"Come on, boss, if it's not a hand-picked mercenary hired by the old man then it's gotta be a local cop," Lincoln said. "Someone that knows patrol patterns, has access to parole data bases, and knows all the players-"

"Barnes is built like a brick shithouse," Morgan said, slamming his empty glass down on the table. "One cop wasn't kicking this guy's ass. Maybe three or four cops, but not one."

"What about Tommy Wilson, huh?" Lincoln asked. "He's been jacked up on 'roids for years. We've all seen him in full roid rage in the locker room. He's capable-"

"You've had a bug up your ass for Wilson for years, since he broke your nose at that Christmas party," Morgan snapped. "Let it go already, Skip."

"He didn't break it," Lincoln replied. "I had a deviated septum."

"Let it go, Skippy."

"A cop hit squad, maybe?" Sammy interjected again. "Like in that Clint Eastwood movie from the 70's?"

Morgan and Lincoln both shot Sammy looks of annoyance.

"Come on guys, that was a great movie," he said defensively. "The end where he blows up the chief's car? Hey, it could happen."

"Do me a favor, Lincoln," Morgan said as he stood to leave, ignoring Sammy's rant. "Don't go mentioning any of this on your stupid blob tonight. Give it a couple days so it's not so friggin' obvious any of that horse crap coming out of your mouth is coming from me, okay?"

"It's called a blog, but you have my word."

"Oh, and one more thing," the lieutenant said as he reached the back door. "Change your socks and wash your ass."

"Hey," Lincoln shouted. "That's two things."

"What Harbor City's Finest won't tell you is that a degenerate rapist caught the beating of a lifetime tonight as he attacked a woman in a dark alley. They won't tell you the sleazebag was paroled by King McSorley during his pandemic-induced, get out of jail free party. They won't tell you that this low-life has no serious connection to the other four upstanding citizens that were murdered. So why was this one was allowed to live? Why spare his life? A lot of questions with no answers…yet.

Adios from the streets we surrendered.

-Bluewave.com

Keith Lincoln finished his early morning crime beat blog as the sun rose over the city's grey skyline. He stretched and rubbed his tired eyes when he heard a knock on his apartment door. He opened it without a word, anticipating her arrival.

"Damn, you look like death warmed over." Charlene Orlow, a tall, statuesque brunette with piercing green eyes stood in the doorway, studying her overly fatigued friend.

"Nice to see you too, my love."

"Oh, don't go and get all offended now," she said as she walked into the apartment and placed her purse on the old leather couch. "I'm just sayin' you need some sleep. Up all night, chasing down ghosts…" Her voice trailed off as she read the words on his desktop computer screen nearby. "A rapist this time, huh? Goddam, this city is a nightmare."

"Don't read that stuff, babe," he said as he handed her a beer from the refrigerator along with a one-hundred-dollar bill. "It'll give you nightmares."

"That's why you don't sleep," Charlene asked as she took a swig. "You're out all night, chasing down these creepy-ass stories. That why you stopped being a cop? Get sick of seeing this shit all the time?"

Lincoln grabbed the woman's hand without a word and quickly led her into the bedroom. Charlene went into the bathroom to strip down to her red lace lingerie. When she stepped out, Lincoln was flat on his back atop the bed, snoring like a lumberjack.

"I'm not sure why I bother," she sighed. "But the money's good. So there's that."

4

"Nice ride," the man said as he looked out the window of the nine seat Cessna Citation CJ3. "Your driver, what's his name again? He's a pilot, too?"

"I purchased it recently, as it became obvious flight is going to continue to be restricted for some time due to these ludicrous virus mandates," Winston replied. "Ernest is multi-talented and multi-faceted. Military background, like you. Special forces, again, as yourself. Followed a different path then you, however."

"Nothing wrong with my path, except a corrupt District Attorney," the man replied, his annoyance evident.

"As you were the lead investigator into my wife's death, I made sure to learn everything I could about you," Winston said, sipping from a small cup of tea on the tray next to his seat. "Obviously I wanted only the finest detective trying to find and put away those that took my beloved away from me. I needed to know if you were up to the task."

"I found them, and I built a rock solid, slam dunk case against those four," the man responded. "It was McSorley and his hand-picked D.A. who let them walk, twice."

"We're both well aware who is responsible," Winston nodded, leaning his head back and closing his eyes. "You did a fine job, lived up to my expectations."

"Well I'm thrilled to hear that, but they still-"

"West Point grad, top of your class," Winston announced, the details rolling off his tongue. "Army Ranger, 2nd Battalion, 75th Ranger Regiment. Silver Star and Purple Heart recipient. First grade Detective, Harbor City Police Department. Divorced, no children."

The man sat quietly, unimpressed by his own resume.

"Terminated, for allegedly planting evidence on one of the suspects." Winston said.

"It was a good collar, good police work," the man replied wistfully. "You know it, everybody knew it. McSorley had Flagg in his pocket and they made me the fall guy. That was bull-"

"I know exactly what it was," Winston said, reopening his eyes. "I know whatever happened ended your career, just as your ensuing bout with depression and alcoholism ended your marriage."

The man stood, his face reddening and his fists and jaw clenched. "I don't have to listen to any more of this crap. You never said my personal life would be a part of this."

"You, my friend, are a fallen angel," Winston smiled, ignoring the man's angry outburst.

"What the hell are you talking about?"

"Human, undone by weakness and circumstance. But that does not extinguish the warrior that once lived inside of you. That is what I am looking to reawaken, to unleash."

The man leaned forward, nearly coming nose to nose with the billionaire. "You don't know shit about me," he growled. "I'm no longer interested in your ridiculous plan. Now have your man servant land this hunk of crap and let me off."

"Twelve hundred dollar a month alimony, seven hundred forty dollars currently in one of your checking accounts, a negative balance in the other. No savings account to speak of, and a credit rating of five hundred thirty-two and trending downwards, quickly."

"You really think you can motivate me through money, Charlie?"

"Heaven's no," Winston answered as the man backed away from him. "I wouldn't dream of it. Money can't buy the loyalty I'm looking for. That must live inside your heart, your soul. The money will afford you certain resources, and help you move on with your life once we are done."

"We're already done."

Winston motioned toward the empty chair. "Please, take a seat, and fasten your seatbelt. There will be some turbulence ahead, I assure you."

Reluctantly, the man sat back down, the veins in his forehead still pulsating. "This is all a joke. It won't work. For God's sake, you still haven't even told me where we're going."

Winston smiled broadly. "Are you familiar with the pandemic in Afro Eurasia in 1346?"

Lincoln smirked as he shook his head in disbelief. "You've gotta be kidding, right?"

Over the next fifteen hours the men shared little conversation, as both fell in and out of consciousness during the fifteen-hour trek. They finally landed at Ben Gurion International Airport, Israel's busiest airfield located twenty-eight miles north of Jerusalem. The groggy duo stepped off the plane into the blinding sunlight and ninety-seven-degree temperature.

"Israel?" the man asked as they walked toward the airport gate. "Seriously? I thought we were going to Maui?"

"We are headed to Mount Tabor, and the Church of the Transformation," Winston said as he placed a white sun visor atop his head. "It is your destiny."

"My destiny? Here?"

"Not by birth," Winston said. "Not at all. But by anointment, soon enough."

"You need psychiatric help, Charlie."

Ernest gathered the men's luggage and met them out near the main parking area. "Our transportation should be arriving momentarily, sir," he said with a wink.

"I hope we're not taking a shuttle bus," the man said, seemingly annoyed by every detail of this unforeseen journey. "I hate shuttle buses. I feel like a damn tourist in Disney World on those things. All I need is a camera, a map, and sun block on my nose."

A muffled roar sounded in the distance, a low growl growing closer by the second. The three men watched as a dark, speeding bullet approached at an incredible rate of speed, finally slowing before coming to a smoldering stop at their feet.

"Jesus friggin' Christ," the man said, his mouth agape as he looked over the jet-black sports car. "What the hell is this, a Lamborghini?"

"Please do not insult me," Winston frowned with disgust. "This, young man, is a Bugatti Chiron. Eight-liter, sixteen cylinder, fifteen hundred horsepower masterpiece. Top speed, two hundred and eighty miles per hour. Not your average shuttle bus, is it?"

"Wow," the man admired the high-performance vehicle, sliding his fingers along its sleek design. "This had to cost, what, a couple hundred grand?"

"I picked two up from a friend out here at a discount. Professional courtesy. The other is back home. Just under three million dollars each."

"Three million?" the man gasped. "When can I drive it?"

"Never!" Winston fired back, looking over at his loyal chauffeur, pilot, and all-around assistant. "Shall we, Ernest?"

5

"Big, bad Benny Barnes," Lieutenant Morgan said as he took a seat next to the hospitaL bed occupied by the badly injured man handcuffed to the gurney. "Former member of the East Side Elite motorcycle gang, now running with the Bianchi family. Six priors, all violent felonies pled down by our illustrious judicial system and District Attorney Flagg. Tell me, Benny, why would a big, ole' smelly stink bug like you pick on a ninety-pound waitress?"

"Go screw yourself, Morgan," Barnes said as he winced in pain, his right arm and left leg in casts. "I'll walk on this, too."

"I've got me a victim who wants to see your balls cut off," Morgan said, smiling. "Maybe we can get the courts to settle for a finger, or an ear. Not really sure how these things are gonna go, you know?"

"She ain't gonna testify against me and you know it," Barnes said confidently. "If you're here looking for a confession, you're wastin' your time, cop."

Morgan scribbled into his note pad, fully aware the smug suspect was right. Someone like Keisha not only feared the city's criminal element, but they also feared the weak-kneed prosecutor whose plea deals put dangerous felons back on the streets within hours. As a cop, he knew the battle was all but lost, yet he promised to keep pushing until the very last minute of his last shift.

"So, who did this to you? Who put big, bad Benny Barnes in the hospital, looking like a mashed-up ole' meatball?"

"Never saw him. I don't know anything."

"You can drop the street code, Benny. Whoever this is, he's coming after you people, and hard. I know you and Bernard Williams were running girls out of the gym on Thirty Sixth. You know he's dead, right? As dead as Teddy Roosevelt's grandmother. Along with his other three pals that killed Anna Winston. Friends of yours?"

"I didn't have nothin' to do with that. No idea what you're talkin' about."

"Come on, Benny. Rival gang, maybe? West Side Wheels? El Gregorios?"

"You know better than that, Morgan. My boss controls everyone. No one moves on anyone without approval from the boss."

"Yeah, I've heard that. I think maybe it's time your boss and I have a sit down."

"If the boss don't wanna talk to you, you ain't gettin' a chair at the table so keep walking, old man."

"His people keep winding up dead or worse, looking like you, he'll talk to me."

Morgan closed his notepad and began to leave the room, when he heard Barnes mumble something inaudible under his breath.

"You say something, dumbass?" the lieutenant asked.

"His eyes," Barnes whispered. "Like the devil."

Morgan stepped back towards the gurney. "Go on."

Barnes shook his head. "No, no more. Just pray you never have to look into them."

Morgan felt a chill run up his spine. It wasn't often that a hardened criminal like Barnes admitted fear, and it was clear whoever had done this to him had left an indelible mark as psychological as he had physical. Still, he had little to go on other than Barnes' murmurings. Once again frustrated by the lack of progress, he headed over to the West Side to see the only other person in Harbor City with more of a finger to the city's pulse than he. He knocked on Keith Lincoln's door and was met by Charlene, her hair messed and wearing only a men's white, button-down dress shirt.

"You wear his clothes?" Morgan asked incredulously. "Goddam, woman! The guy doesn't have crabs, he's got lobsters!"

Charlene rolled her eyes and stepped aside as the lieutenant walked in, finding Lincoln sprawled out naked on his king-size mattress. "Good God! My eyes! At least put a damn towel on, Skippy!"

Lincoln yawned and stretched before reaching for a soiled pair of jeans nearby. He threw them on, reached into his front pocket and took out a wad of crumpled cash. "Here you go, babe," he said, handing the money to Charlene. "You deserve a bonus."

"You're a hopeless romantic." Charlene kissed him, winked at Morgan, and walked out of the bedroom.

"Sickening," Morgan said as he admired the woman's ultra-sexy walk. "But definitely one of your better ones. Where'd you find her?"

"She just walked up to me at Sweeney's Bar last week and started talking. We're getting married next month. Oh, and you're invited."

"Well then, I'd make sure there's some venereal disease tests before the nuptials." Morgan said.

Lincoln shook his head. "Nah, she's clean."

"I was talking about you, jackass."

"Oh," Lincoln grinned. "There a reason you're here before noon and didn't bring food?"

Morgan paced back and forth. "The perp from the rape last night, Benny Barnes."

Lincoln threw a t-shirt over his head and walked into the nearby bathroom. "Sure, East Side Elite's. Bad bunch of hombres. You'd have to be crazy to pick a fight with one of them, especially since they're now protected by The Family."

"Yeah, Benny's a made man, and whoever drop kicked his ass didn't seem to care."

"Maybe whoever didn't know?"

"Not a chance," Morgan replied, kicking a dirty, discarded sock under the man's bed. "Everyone who's been hit has been a McSorley parolee. Maybe it's no longer about the

Winston murder, maybe it's somebody out on a revenge mission against McSorley."

"Could be anyone who despises that incompetent moron," Lincoln surmised. "Cops, victims, politicians on the other side of the fence."

"You." Morgan said.

Lincoln looked over at the lieutenant and smiled. "I hate the bastard and I certainly have motive, but I've moved on."

"Yeah, and you probably couldn't stay sober long enough to kick my Aunt Millie's ass, so I guess I'll eliminate you as a suspect. But you think it's a cop, right? You spewing that theory on your blob?"

"For the one millionth time it's called a blog, not a blob," Lincoln said as he began brushing his teeth. "And yeah, that's what I'm thinking."

Morgan crossed his arms in front of him. "Well, I could get Internal Affairs involved, but the cops will just stone wall them. You know every cop on this job and they know you. They'll talk to you, off the record."

Lincoln spit into the sink and wiped his mouth with his shirt. "Some will, others will tell me to screw off and die. To some I'm still a cop, to others I'm a disgrace who now spills secrets on the internet."

"The good cops love what you do. The cranky-ass bosses, the bad apples, yeah I could see them putting your head in a vice and tightening it until your eyeballs explode against the wall like old, rotten blueberries. The ones in the discount bins, you know, that are too ripe."

Lincoln peered out of the bathroom. "Huh?"

"Doesn't matter," Morgan said. "Look, Skip, I need your help. I can't have whoever this is running around at night attacking people in the street, even if they are stinkin' bags of cow crap. Eventually you-know-who is gonna put a price on this dude's head, and that's when innocent people get caught in the crossfire."

"Maybe that's what he wants," Lincoln said as he spun around, searching the bedroom floor. "Maybe this cop turned vigilante wants a piece of the big man himself. Draw him out. By the way, did you happen to see my other sock?"

"Yeah, I called the Center for Disease Control and donated it to science."

"I'll talk to some of my closer contacts, see what the word is. I'll get back to you in a couple days."

"Don't take too long," Morgan said as he turned to leave. "Your liver could explode at any minute, like a watermelon dropped from the eighteenth floor of the Hilton. Tell me I'm wrong?"

Lincoln laughed. "Hard to argue."

There is one thing that's bugging me." Morgan said quietly. "Barnes described his attacker as having eyes like the devil. That mean anything to you?"

Lincoln paused for a moment before answering. "Well, Barnes could have been drunk off his ass…"

"No, doc at the hospital said he was sober when they brought him in."

"Okay, then I guess you've got a vampire problem out there, lieutenant."

Morgan sneered. "You were born stupid, weren't you?"

6

"What is this place?"

CharleS Winston and Ernest stayed silent as the three men finished their trek high above Mount Tabor. The ancient church stood before them, a limestone façade of two projecting towers between a round-headed arch that framed the historical complex overlooking the hills of Nazareth to the west, the West Bank to the south, the Jordan rift valley to the east, and Galilee to the north.

"Amazing," the man said as they entered, a gorgeous, golden mosaic illuminated by the sun's rays striking a glass plate in the church's floor. "But what is it, and why are we here?"

"The Church of the Transfiguration," Winston said, still in awe of the fascinating architecture even after a recent visit to the holy site. "It is here that Jesus Christ spoke with Moses and Elijah, where God referred to him as 'son.' When Christ became the preeminent figure of Judaism, and when God made it clear his son was to be followed and listened to."

"Fascinating," the man said, truly moved by the structure and the view. "But if I recall correctly, Jesus ended up getting crucified."

Winston shook his head. "If you follow and invest your will and your soul into our mission, then you and only you can dictate your destiny."

The man nodded, blowing off Winston's whimsical response. He continued to admire the sprawling cathedral and spectacular works inside of it, before turning back to the billionaire. "So, I'm guessing this is where you will try to transfigure me? Damn, that sounded creepy as hell."

"Precisely," Winston said with an ear-to-ear grin. "Here we will hone your long dormant skills, bringing them to levels few humans have ever reached, while instilling some you never knew possible. You will learn from the master himself and emerge transfigured."

"You've piqued my interest," the man said. "When does this master of yours get here?"

The man felt a sudden, gripping pain on the back of his neck, his legs buckling under him as he fell helplessly to the church floor. He grimaced in pain as he rolled onto his side, looking up at Winston's chauffeur towering over him.

"Ernest spent decades training Navy Seals in several arts, one of which you just experienced. I know that may not sit well with you Army Ranger boys, but there's no one better on the planet. I suggest you pay close attention and be a good student during our time here."

The man shook off the pain and rose to his feet, now standing toe to toe with the much larger Ernest. "That was a goddam cheap shot, Ernie. Look me in the eye, Navy boy, and then-"

Ernest unleashed two lightning-fast strikes to the sternum that knocked the man back several feet, and followed with a kick to the right shoulder that sent him spinning and sprawling across the floor.

"I failed to mention Ernest is also a tenth-degree black belt in judo, one of only a handful across the globe," Winston said, his grin somehow expanding. "He can permanently disable you, or terminate you if need be, but that's not our goal here."

His right arm dangling at his side, the man clutched his aching shoulder and struggled to his feet. "If he's so damn good, why don't you use him to play your stupid game?"

Winston shook his head. "Ernest is a teacher now, a professor. At this stage of his life, it's about passing on his knowledge. A passing of the torch, you might say. Besides, who would go to the store and pick out my fresh vegetables?"

"Oh yeah, good point." The man grunted before lunging forward toward Ernest's throat. The master side-stepped the attack, allowing the student to stumble before falling to the ground face first.

"Welcome to the first day of your training." Winston said.

"How am I doing so far?," the man wheezed as he lay prone, his vision blurred as he looked up at a gorgeous statue of Jesus Christ on the cross. "Just give me a moment to catch my breath and I'll kick your ass, Ernie."

Keith Lincoln sat alone on the wooden bench, looking out toward the towering lighthouse that illuminated the harbor. All was quiet on another hot, humid night, only the usual drunkards and homeless inhabiting the once bustling, scenic promenade. He scratched at his four-day old stubble, running his hands through his hair as he tried to stay awake while awaiting his visitor. At a quarter past midnight, the blue and white Harbor PD cruiser pulled up, the vagrants scattering, expecting to be shuffled off to another, less-visible location.

Out of the car stepped Tom Wilson, a twenty-five-year veteran of the force and one of the toughest street cops Harbor City had ever seen. Wilson stood six foot five and was a rock solid two hundred and thirty pounds, with a chiseled jaw that had taken its fair share of punches in the streets and local bars. He was a former amateur boxer with a 17-2 overall record and had never been shy about using his skills on those that challenged him on the street or in the watering holes. He took a seat on the bench next to Lincoln and looked up toward the stars.

"Tell me something, blog boy," Wilson said, his Chicago-area accent hard to miss. "When they kicked you off this job, why didn't you just keep walking? Why stick around and play this whistleblower bullshit?"

"Someone has to let people know what really goes on in this city," Lincoln said with a yawn. "You guys can't speak up, so I do it for you. You're welcome, by the way."

"Well, most cops think you're a hero, but there are those who wanna smash a beer bottle over your head."

Lincoln laughed. "And which group do you fall in?"

Wilson crossed his massive arms across his chest. "We've been there before, haven't we?"

"Yeah, I guess so," Lincoln replied. "Look, Morgan is chasing his tail trying to find whoever has been targeting the Winston suspects. I'm trying to help him out."

"Trying to help him, or trying to get more eyeballs on your website?" Wilson asked cynically. "So you can clean up your name, right?"

"All of the above."

"Look, all we know is every time we pull up on a scene, these pieces of crap are already DOA or beat to shit, and no one's around. Not one sector car has ever been in the area when one of these beat downs have occurred. Coincidence?"

"So you and I are on the same page," Lincoln surmised. "A cop, or cops, who know the sector's normal patrol routes, routines, when they're tied up on a job somewhere else…"

"Yeah, it's pretty obvious. The only question is, who? If it's just one cop, who's capable of delivering beat downs like this? And if it's a bunch of guys, how the hell are they keeping it quiet? Cops are like bored housewives. No way in hell they can keep something like this under wraps too long."

Lincoln stared at Wilson, a little too long for the veteran street cops' liking.

"Me? Kiss my ass, Lincoln," the big man growled. "I'm too damn old and unmotivated to pull something like this off."

"You sure about that? I saw what you did to Sid Cosby at Houlihan's a few months ago."

"Sid Cosby is a rat bastard," Wilson snapped. "I'm not the only guy who wanted to kick his whiny ass, I'm only the first one to actually do it. That don't mean I'm running around at night beating ex-cons to death for fun."

Lincoln nodded in agreement. "Once again, fair point. What's being said in the locker room?"

Wilson laughed. "Listen, everyone knows it's McSorley's call, direct from City Hall. No one goes near old man Winston and no one talks to the press or even you, for that matter. You don't honestly believe for one second Mayor Mac wants this stuff getting publicity, do you? His bailouts getting taken out one by one? Nah, all just coincidences. So we show up, call an ambulance, take a report and roll to the next job."

"McSorley better be careful," Lincoln said. "Whoever's doing this might target him next."

"McSorley's a first grade idiot, but he's not stupid. He doubled his security detail. City Hall, his townhouse? Goddam fortresses right now. No one can get near him. No one."

Lincoln stood and extended his hand. "As always, you've proven to be absolutely useless to me."

"Go home and sober up, Lincoln. Leave the police work to us real cops."

"So why has Harbor City's illustrious Mayor beefed up his security at his office and at his home? Is it because he knows the truth; that someone, or some people, are going after the ex-cons he released, starting with the four who killed Anna Winston? Is he worried that he may be on their list, possibly even next? What about D.A. Flagg? If so, why isn't McSorley telling anyone what those in police circles already know? That his post-virus, let-em-loose policies and laughable prosecution are coming back to bite his bureaucratic ass in a way he never could have imagined.

"DA Flagg, are you paying attention?"

Sleep well, Harbor City. The fun is just beginning.

Bluewave.com

###

Marty McSorley sat at a table in the dim, far corner of The Quarter House, a German restaurant that up until the pandemic had been one of Harbor City's most bustling eateries. Now, it suffered, on the brink of closure as its owner contemplated leaving his livelihood behind and heading south toward the business-friendly Florida coast.

The mayor's police detail stepped away from the front door to allow District Attorney Arturo 'Art" Flagg to enter. Flagg, who next to McSorley had become the most unpopular of the City's politicians, wore dark glasses and an oversized, out-of-season coat to conceal his identity as he took a seat next to the mayor. Physically, McSorley and Flagg were complete opposites; the mayor tall and gangly at six foot five and one hundred and seventy pounds, the District Attorney short, stocky and about twenty pounds overweight. Politically, they adhered to the same criminal- sympathizing ideologies.

"Are you sure your detail can stop this guy if he comes looking for us?" Flagg asked nervously as he eyeballed the seven detectives near the door. "I'm not sure meeting out in public like this is a good idea, especially at night, Marty."

"Calm down, Art," McSorley said. "If he comes within fifty feet of us, my detail will put him down."

"If that's the case, why are you shaking like a lost schoolgirl?" Flagg asked, pointing to McSorley's trembling hands

McSorley pulled his hands off the table and buried them under his thighs. "I keep telling you, Art, he's not the one we have to worry about. He's just some nutcase carrying out Charlie Winston's orders, that's all."

"You're sure about that?" Flagg asked.

"Yes, but as you well know, we can't get close to Charlie without creating huge waves. We finger him as a person of interest and our stocks will crumble in minutes. Charlie Winston keeps this entire state functioning. Let him take out those ex-cons and have his little revenge party. Doesn't affect us. However-"

"The cop and his website," Flagg said, removing his glasses and toying nervously with the silverware in front of him. "That's who you're worried about?"

McSorley nodded. "Ex-cop. He's our real problem. He's getting information from someone on the inside for a while now. He's obsessed with whoever this vigilante nutcase is. We've kept a lid on the media coverage but he just can't shut his mouth. This is all your fault."

"My fault?" Flagg fired back indignantly. "How the hell did you come to that conclusion?"

"You said he was finished after your office charged him with perjury and I fired him on your recommendation. You assured me-"

"I thought he would," McSorley shrugged. "A cop fired for planting evidence, marriage falling apart…they usually fade away pretty quickly. Too much shame and embarrassment. Lincoln hit the bottle hard and started this ridiculous website, thinking he'd be some knight in shining armor for the good citizens of Harbor City. Have to admit, I thought we'd find him dead in an alley by now."

"Well, he's not dead, and he's causing trouble. He's got a lot of followers who are starting to believe his bullshit. They believe your office set him up."

Flagg's uneasy silence spoke volumes.

"Jesus Christ," McSorley sighed heavily. "I don't want to know."

Flagg rolled his eyes and checked his watch.

"Never mind. I'll deal with Keith Lincoln," the mayor growled, growing more and more agitated with Flagg by the second. "You just keep your shit together and start throwing me some more fundraisers. We're going to need every dollar. If I don't get reelected, both our careers are over. Am I being clear?"

Flagg nodded as he stood. "Crystal clear, Mr. Mayor." He headed for the door and his waiting Cadillac, pausing before exiting. "One has-been cop can't unnerve you like this. Be honest with yourself, Marty. It's the vigilante. He can bring the whole damn house down on both of us. Your police department needs to stop him, by any means necessary. I knew this was a bad idea. All of it, from the very beginning." He quickly made his way out the door and into his car. McSorley stayed behind, tapping his cell phone and placing it to his ear.

"Set up a meeting with Lieutenant Morgan from the Eastern District," he said quietly. "I'd like to talk to him."

7

The knock at the door just past dawn startled him, his tired eyes checking the clock on the night table as he stumbled out of the bedroom. He swung open the door and found the diminutive female in her dark blue uniform standing in the hallway.

"What the hell do you want?" Lincoln asked groggily. "Another loud sex complaint? Nosy ass neighbors need to mind their business."

"I saw him," said the jittery cop. "Well, I saw something tonight. It was him. It had to be."

"What?" Lincoln asked as he rubbed his eyes and yawned. "Who? What? Go away, crazy lady."

Police Officer Linda Esperanza pushed past Lincoln and into his dark apartment. The ten-year veteran stood just five feet tall, but overcame any size limitations with her hair-trigger temper and reputation for being one tough street cop. The dark-skinned, hot-blooded single mother removed her eight-point cap and pulled at her pony tail, her long, jet-black hair tied up neatly atop her head.

"Yeah, sure. Come on in," Lincoln said sarcastically. "Make yourself at home."

"It was him, the guy we're looking for."

Lincoln walked slowly into the kitchen area and turned on the wall switch, squinting as the bright light hit his bloodshot eyes. "You saw him? Like, really saw him? You're not drinking again, are you Linda? I thought you were sobering up?"

"Screw you, Lincoln. I stopped drinking after we stopped being partners. Coincidence?"

"Probably not," he said as he removed a half-empty bottle of white zinfandel from his refrigerator. "But at least I can admit I have a problem. You, on the other hand-"

"You gonna listen to me or keep being an asshole all your life?"

Lincoln put the bottle down and looked sideways at the cop. "You're serious, aren't you?"

"I was working Sector Adam with Hutchinson-"

"Hutchinson?" Lincoln interrupted. "Tall blonde guy, wants to be a country singer but sucks at karaoke?"

"Would you shut your goddam, stupid mouth and listen to me?" she snapped. "About four hours ago, around one thirty, we get flagged down by some street walker who says she saw something, wasn't sure if it was a car or a goddam rocket ship, but it tore down Sutter Avenue behind the old used clothing store. We took a ride to check it out and that's when we saw Tony Tolbert and some other guy huddled near a garage."

"Tony Tolbert?" Lincoln asked. "The meth dealer?"

"Yep, that's the guy. We figured we had ourselves a nice possession and distribution collar, when Tolbert sees us and bolts. We split up, Hutchinson went after the buyer and I went after Tolbert. He ran down South Tenth and cut across Sutter. He's a lot friggin' faster than he looks. I was about fifty feet behind him when all of a sudden this thing jumps out of the dark."

"Thing?" Lincoln raised an eyebrow. "Can you be a little more specific?"

"No, I can't," she replied. "It was just something in the dark. It lifted Tolbert's ass right off the ground. His feet were dangling in the air like a goddam fish! He hung in midair there for a minute before falling to the ground. What a sound it made. I'll never forget that."

"Jesus," Lincoln said, his demeanor turning serious. "And you didn't see his face or anything?"

"His eyes. All I saw were two red eyes that looked like they were on fire or something."

"Like the devil?" Lincoln asked, remembering what Benny Barnes had said to Lieutenant Morgan. "Satanic looking?"

"Yeah," Linda replied softly, the image clear in her mind. "Scary as hell."

"Did this thing see you?" Lincoln asked. "Does he know you saw him?"

"Not sure," Linda answered as she began pacing back and forth. "Now I can't stop shaking."

Lincoln walked over to a beige loveseat and sat down. "He probably wanted you to see him; someone to see him. He had to know you were there. There hasn't been one damn witness before this, now all of a sudden he's putting on a show for the cops? If he didn't want to be seen, he wouldn't have. He's sending a message."

"What's his message?" Linda asked, her hands trembling. "That he scared me shitless?"

"It's gotta be Tommy Wilson. Was he at work tonight?"

"No, at least I didn't see him at roll call."

"Okay, listen. You stay far away from this, you understand? You see him again, or don't see him again, you get three or four cars over there right away. Don't go playing hero."

"Not a chance," Linda said as she took a seat next to him. "No way. I'm sorry I woke you. I just needed to talk."

"So you came to the one man in Harbor City you trust, right?"

"Trust you? That might be the stupidest thing you've ever said, and that's saying something. You were a great cop and a great partner, but after everything went down with the Winston case, you fell apart, man. You just gave up."

"Thanks for your support," Lincoln joked. "I'm better now, though. Cutting down on the drinking, swore off women…"

"Oh really?" Linda said as she reached for the whistle on her gun belt, placing it in her mouth and blowing into it.

"What the hell is wrong with you?" Lincoln asked as he held his hands over his ears. "The neighbors will freak."

"You really think I don't smell that cheap whore perfume all over you?"

Lincoln held his t-shirt up to his nose. "That's fabric softener, I'll have you know."

Out of the bedroom walked a heavy-set, bosomy blonde, wearing only what appeared to be Lincoln's stretched out red and blue boxers. Her hair and makeup a mess, she trudged over to where the couple sat and held out her hand. Lincoln reached inside his shorts and pulled out a crumpled fifty-dollar bill, handing it to the grateful woman. "Thanks, Greta. Safe home. Sorry about the dog whistle."

"Call me," she said as she headed back to the bedroom to retrieve her clothing.

"What?" Lincoln asked, shrugging his shoulders while acknowledging his former partners disapproving glare. "She's my cleaning lady."

"Really?" Linda looked around the room filled with dirty clothes and empty Chinese food cartons. "You should fire her immediately."

"Good help is hard to find."

"So how's Abby?" Linda asked, touching on a delicate subject. "Talk to her lately?"

"She's fine." Lincoln mumbled before steering the conversation away from his ex-wife. "Does Morgan know about this?"

"Down at the crime scene now," she said as she began to leave. "Fifty bucks, huh? Last of the big-time spenders."

Lincoln reached back into his pocket. "Don't go anywhere. I may have another twenty on me."

Linda shook her head. "Save it. Buy yourself some new socks."

8

"Tell your boss I need to talk to him, pronto."

The large, muscular man standing guard at the rear entrance to Lena's Italian Bistro glared at the man making demands and laughed. "Pronto? Is that supposed to make me move? Take a walk, you crazy old man."

Lieutenant Morgan pulled back his brown sports coat, revealing the gold shield attached to his belt. "This crazy old man will kick your steroid ass up and down Fifth Avenue if you don't step aside, Skippy."

The man laughed again. "You're serious? You think that badge gets you a sit down with the boss?"

"You tell your boss it's Morgan. Yeah, the cop who locked his gangster ass up fifteen years ago. That'll get his attention."

"You're clueless, and a bit late to the party," The man smirked as he motioned for the cop to wait outside as he slipped inside the door. Several minutes later he reappeared, ordering Morgan to disarm before entry.

"I'm a goddam lieutenant of police!" Morgan protested. "I'm not turning my gun over to no sleazy stink bug like you!"

The man shrugged. "No guns. Boss' orders. Otherwise, have a good night, lieutenant of police."

"Don't mock me, Skippy," Morgan said as he begrudgingly un-holstered the nine-millimeter on his hip and placed it in the man's giant hand. "I'll put a size ten foot up your dopey ass."

"The one on your ankle, too."

"Goddam it, you brain dead, punching bag," Morgan fumed as he removed the .38 caliber revolver from his left leg. "Out of my way."

Morgan was led through the empty, glitzy eatery to a back room, where three men even larger than the one he encountered outside stood around an oval shaped, marble table. They glared as they sized him up, with palpable disdain for his supposed authority within the city.

"I ain't got time for games," Morgan said as he glared back at the imposing men, pointing at the largest of the trio. "Franco, right? Didn't I lock your ass up a few years ago for petty larceny? You still stealin' candy bars off the shelves, tough guy?"

Franco Toscano, a lieutenant in the Bianchi crime family, ignored the slight. A door creaked in the darkness, footsteps approaching. Morgan strained to get a better look at Harbor City's longtime organized crime boss. The silhouette in the darkness certainly did not match that of a seventy-year-old, short and overweight man. Instead, it looked more like…

"Who the hell are you?" Morgan said to the statuesque brunette standing before him. "No, wait. It can't be. Erica?"

Erica Bianchi sat down and motioned for Morgan to do the same. When he hesitated, his mouth still wide open, Franco grabbed him by the shoulder and forced him into a chair.

"Jesus," the cop mumbled. "The last time I saw you-"

"I was ten years old," Erica said, crossing her arms and legs simultaneously. "Outside criminal court, during my father's trial, when you helped put him in prison and made me an orphan."

Over the course of forty years, Alfonse Bianchi had risen from Harbor City street thug to the top of the criminal food chain. An old school wise guy, Alfonse believed in the old mafia codes, and was considered a man of respect. He never dabbled in narcotics or prostitution, instead making his illicit fortune through loan sharking, hijacking, gambling and casino management. He revered children and families, avoided confrontations with the police and the FBI at all costs, and led the life of a secluded entrepreneur. His one slip up came when one of his subordinates was collared on a gun charge and, facing a mandatory ten-year sentence as a three-time violator, spilled his guts to a young detective named Clayton Morgan.

"What can I say? Just doing my job back then, little girl. It was a long time ago. No hard feelings, right?"

Morgan's dismissive attitude infuriated Erica, who rose from her seat, reached across the table and grabbed Morgan's tie, yanking him toward her. "You ever refer to me as a little girl again, I will personally slit your throat and watch you bleed out. Are we clear, lieutenant?"

Morgan nodded. "Yeah, sure, Erica. I like my blood right where it is, so no problem with that."

Erica growled and released her hold, Morgan falling back into his chair. He was stunned by the woman's strength, only now noticing her tone, muscular build and chiseled features. She was a stunning beauty, but he realized behind her looks was a very powerful, dangerous woman.

"So, how is your father?" he asked, sheepishly. "I really need to talk to him."

Erica shook her head. "My father was taken from us several months ago. The virus got him. He was weak from all those years in prison. He couldn't fight it off. But his family, this thing of ours, is stronger than ever."

"Wait, how could Alfonse Bianchi die and I not know about it? How could we not know he was sick?"

"We hid him, protected him," Erica said. "If those vultures from Chicago knew he was seriously ill, they would have come after us and destroyed everything he built. I couldn't let that happen. Once our organization stabilized again, under a new capo, we were ready to move on."

"Makes a lotta sense," Morgan said. "So, who's the new capo? Who's the Godfather, or whatever you guys and gals call it nowadays?"

Erica leaned forward and glared at the cop. "I am, you idiot."

"Oh, come on," Morgan laughed. "There's no way on God's green Earth Cosa Nostra would let a woman-"

Erica stood again, her fists and teeth clenched tightly.

"I'm sorry, I'm sorry. My mistake," Morgan said, bowing his head. "I meant no disrespect, God…mother?"

"I built myself into what you see here today, and I rebuilt my father's organization. Now we are stronger than ever. I've united every criminal entity, street gang, and money-making operation in this city under my command, and there's nothing you or the Feds can do about it, lieutenant. I'm sure you realize you have no support from City Hall and the DA. Harbor City is mine."

"Well, okay, but I'm not your problem," Morgan said with a sly grin.

Erica sat down and glared at him, her icy stare unnerving. "You mean, him?"

"Yeah, him. He's flesh and blood, I think, but one spooky sunavabitch. As you well know, he took out four of your mopes who killed Charlie Winston's wife, but he's obviously not done. Benny Barnes? Tony Tolbert? I'm pretty sure those mopes belong to you too."

"You're as blind as I thought," Erica said. "It's being dealt with."

"Blind? Come on, don't blow smoke up my ass and tell me you're cooking smores. You have no idea who he is, where he is, or what he's going to do next. But I can tell you this. It looks like he's working his way through the Bianchi operation, and if you're at the top of the ladder now-"

"So why come to me?" Erica asked, growing more annoyed as the conversation went on. "Are you offering me protection, because that would be both offensive and ludicrous at the same time."

"No, not at all. After the virus, we can barely protect ourselves," Morgan said dejectedly. "I'm here trying to avoid a bloodbath. I know eventually you're going to go after this guy with everything you got till you find him, and I don't want innocent civilians or cops getting caught in the crossfire."

"Unfortunately, it seems that's inevitable, lieutenant."

Frustrated, Morgan placed his head in his hands and sighed. "We can work together, Erica. Share information, get this bastard off the streets before Little Granny Corn Muffin gets gunned down while out for a walk to pick up pickled beets at the grocery store."

Erica stood again, looking down at Morgan. "We'll handle our business, you handle yours. Goodbye, lieutenant. It was not a pleasurable reunion. My associates will show you the door."

"You're making a huge freakin' mistake, Erica," Morgan shouted as two men lifted him off his chair. "You could be next!"

The woman walked around the table to where her men held Morgan by each of his arms. She moved closer, her nose practically touching his, their eyes locked on one another's. Morgan felt a sense of dread run through his body as he stared into her steely, black eyes.

"When my father died, his once-powerful body wracked by pain and disease, that little girl you referred to died as well. I fear no one and will die before anyone tries to take this away from my family. Understood, lieutenant?"

"Okay, but don't go sayin' I didn't warn you."

Erica's glare grew icier. "You want help with this, lieutenant? Remember, land before love. There, I've done my part. Toss him to the curb, gentlemen."

"What the hell does that mean?" Morgan asked, before the men dragged him to the rear door, tossing him out into the street like a bag of garbage. They threw his handguns out near the curb and slammed the door shut behind them.

Morgan wiped the dirt from his torn slacks as he looked back at the door. "Crazy-ass bitch. Land before what? I ain't got time for puzzles, you psycho woman!"

9

The three men exited the church and stood side by side, high atop Mount Tabor looking toward Galilee. The sun beat down upon them, the temperature reaching triple digits. Clad fully in black spandex which accentuated his new lean, muscular physique, the protégé took a few steps forward, and knelt before Charles and Ernest.

His body and mind ached as never before. Even through the Army's rigorous boot camp and the torturous Ranger training, he had never experienced anything close to what he had over the prior two and a half months. Ernest had challenged him, pushing him to limits not even the Army knew he had within him. As he knelt in the raging sun, his head bowed, he knew he had crossed over and become something he never could have imagined. His body was stronger, his mind even more. He was far quicker, more agile than ever. Just as important, he was as focused as humanly possible.

"You have been transfigured," Winston said, looking down upon his project. "You are now no longer just a man. You are wrath. Those that destroyed my city, took my wife from me and ruined your life, will now feel the wrath of God, an affliction far worse than the virus that began our fall."

"Yes," the man said. "They all will."

The wind suddenly began to pick up, warm gusts of air blowing across the hills. Ernest walked toward the man and extended his hand. He took it and rose to his feet feeling more empowered than he could have ever imagined. He looked over toward Winston, the two men exchanging slight nods of acknowledgement.

"Retribution and rebirth," the man said. "I will not let you down."

"Retribution for my broken heart," Winston said. "Rebirth for my city, and for you as well."

Ernest stood tall and proud like a new father, satisfied that he had trained and prepared his latest protégé for the battles ahead. "You are indeed ready for whatever Mr. Winston has in store for you. I am honored to have served you both."

"In 1346, Black Death reigned down upon Eurasia and North Africa, a pandemic so devastating it caused the deaths of nearly two hundred million people," Winston said as he looked into the blinding sun. "It changed the course of history, affecting economics, social standing and religious beliefs. Two years ago, this man-made pandemic did the same, through fear and corrosive politics. It is now time to rain another curse down on those responsible." He reached into a fabric bag slung over his shoulder and removed a black mask, placing it over the man's head, fully concealing his identity and displaying a frightening set of demonic eyes. "It is time to unleash something they will all dread, something far worse than anything they've encountered before."

"And that is?" the man asked.

"You," Winston said. "The Black Plague."

###

Clayton Morgan eyeballed the Mayor as he slowly walked into the City Hall office, trying to hide his disdain for McSorley and any and all things politics. He sat down and looked past the Mayor through the large window behind him, the city skyline as grey and depressed as he had ever seen it.

"So, how goes the investigation?" McSorley asked, bypassing any welcoming pleasantries. "Any leads, any informants giving you info? I know you've been around a long time, am I correct?"

Morgan cringed. "Yes, your honor. Thirty years at the end of this month, and if you're talking about the investigation into the murders of the four men who were suspects in the Anna Winston homicide, and the two assaults that followed, the answer's a big fat nope. I've got nothing."

"That's disappointing, to say the least," McSorley said with a frown. "But that's not the only reason I called you here today. What do you know about this whistleblower website?"

Morgan shrugged. "No idea what you're talking about."

"Really?" McSorley said. "Surprising, since I'm told every cop and their mother follows it. This Keith Lincoln is some crusader, isn't he?"

Morgan shook his head. "Again, I have no idea-"

"Stop playing games with me, Lieutenant, or you'll find there's no pension waiting for you when we put you out to pasture. I've been told its Lincoln, the disgraced detective who dishonored the badge and almost ruined the lives of those four young men he tried to railroad. I know you worked with him. Now tell me what you know? Who's talking to him, Lieutenant?"

"Your honor, with all due respect," Morgan said as he climbed out of the chair. "You aren't the sharpest knife in the drawer, are you?"

McSorley's face turned fire engine red as his blood boiled. "What the hell did you just say to me?"

"Here you are, worried about a stupid blob written by a fall down, drunken man-whore who nobody gives a camel's shit about, when you should be worried about how the Bianchi family is going to respond to their boys gettin' whacked in the street."

"I think it's called a blog, Lieutenant, and the Bianchi family has handled their own business in this city for decades without anyone outside their circle getting hurt. Alfonse Bianchi is a man of honor and old school respect. A legitimate businessman."

"Alfonse ain't calling the shots anymore, your eminence," Morgan sneered. "The new boss could give a rats' ass about honor and respect."

McSorley looked confused. "What are you talking about? What new boss?"

Morgan laughed as he turned toward the door. "There's a lot you don't know. Maybe you should hire a detective."

"Maybe I should fire a lieutenant instead!" McSorley fired back.

"Land before love, your highness," Morgan quipped. "Land before love."

"Now what the hell does that mean?"

"I have no idea," replied Morgan as he strutted out of the office like a prancing peacock. "I was kinda hoping you knew."

10

"So, we are done, right?"

The Black Plague vigilante stood at attention, awaiting Charles Winston's acknowledgement. The billionaire instead stared out his window, undoubtedly studying the clouds for images of his wife. After nearly twenty seconds of silence had passed, the man asked again.

"Our mission is complete, correct?"

Winston turned and looked at his creation with surprise. "What on Earth are you talking about?"

The man turned to look at Ernest, wondering if he was not being let in on an inside joke. "Am I missing something? I handled those four, which was my job. We diverted attention away from you with the last two targets, and though I still think I should have killed them like the others, I understand. We've got McSorley running scared. You got your revenge and I'm a new man. Retribution and rebirth, right? That was the mission, as I understood it."

Winston walked over and placed his arm around the man, leading him back toward the window. "Look out there. What do you see?"

The vigilante took a moment before answering. "I see a city that was brought to its knees by corrupt politicians. But I also see a city that can be reborn."

"Do you see the old Harbor City?" Winston asked, as his voice began to rise. "Do you see business booming, children playing in the streets, women walking along the pier near the lighthouse, peering out toward the water without fear of being senselessly murdered by thugs and miscreants? Do you see that yet, sir?"

The man shook his head and cleared his throat. "No, I don't. But-"

"Then explain to me how our mission is complete?" Winston snapped. "You have done such good over these past few weeks, but our journey is just beginning. The element must be fully extinguished for Harbor City to rise and for my Anna to have not died in vain. Besides, the goal is to rid this city of the mayor."

"We're going to kill McSorley now?"

"Heavens no. We are going to rid Harbor City of him the old fashioned, American way. We are going to publicly humiliate him, expose the Big Lie-"

"The big lie?" asked the man.

"In due time. The Big Lie will bring down the castle. We will then put forth a candidate that will defeat him at the polls next November. An honorable, patriotic approach, wouldn't you agree?"

The Black Plague nodded in agreement. There was more to do.

Peter 'Petey Sneaks' Duncan stood nervously on the corner of Banks Avenue and West 12th Street, the dim streetlamps barely illuminating the quiet sidewalks. The man known for his penchant for spending every dime he'd ever earned on new, expensive sneakers looked around at the darkness, his hands fidgeting in his pockets. He cursed himself for accepting the low-level job put upon him by his boss. Ultimately, he knew he had little choice. He could either carry out his assignment or face certain death on the orders of Erica Bianchi.

To his left, a man approached slowly. His eyes not what they used to be, Duncan squinted and strained to make out the man's face. He hoped it was who he was waiting for, and could care less if it was a cop. Over the course of two decades, the now thirty-five-year-old could smell an undercover from a mile away. He prayed, however, that it was not the ghost that everyone in his circles was whispering about.

"Petey Sneaks," the man in the stained grey blazer and torn jeans said as he walked up to the frazzled ex-con. "Been a long time. I see you're still picking up bag drops for the mob. Still can't find a real job, huh?"

Duncan moved closer to get a better look at the man's face. "Holy shit. I heard you were dead."

"Nah, just living the quiet life," Lincoln said with a wink. "Seriously, man, what the hell are you doing out here at two in the morning?"

"Making an honest living, cop," Duncan sneered. "What'd you think, after you busted me I was gonna become a priest or something? Turn over a new leaf? That's fairy tale land. Hollywood bullshit."

"Fair enough. So who are you working for these days? I'm hearing some talk that there's a new boss running things."

Duncan laughed as he wiped his nose with his sleeve. "Look, I ain't got nothin' to say to you, so why don't you just go write some tickets or have a donut somewhere, okay?"

"Not a cop anymore, Petey. I'm an investigative reporter, sort of, the man on the street. I hear it's pretty dangerous out here. Somebody's after McSorley's parolees, and they all seem to be tied in with the Bianchi's. Aren't you a little scared being out here all alone, I mean, being you qualify as both?"

"I ain't scared of nothin'" Duncan said, his jittery body and roaming eyes telling a different story. "Somebody's been feeding you bullshit, Lincoln. Go report that, asshole."

"Just looking for some answers," Lincoln said as he turned away. "If you hear anything, let me know. Nice to see you again, Sneaks. Be careful out here. It's kinda scary."

"Kiss my ass, Lincoln." Duncan watched the former cop walk away, spitting in his direction.

The summer evening wind began to pick up, Duncan checking his watch several times, wondering how much longer he had to wait. He was told very little about the drop, only that an underling was delivering a substantial amount of cash that was to be delivered immediately to Erica upon receipt. He had only met Harbor City's new crime lord once, her piercing eyes intimidating him to the point where he stared at the floor while she spoke. He dreaded another face to face meeting but anticipated her approval once he turned the bag of cash over and completed the job.

"Peter Duncan."

His name whispering through the warm air, Duncan spun around in circles, searching for whomever called out to him. Finding no one in sight, he slammed his open right palm against the right side of his head, trying to shake the strange noises from his scattered mind. He tried to focus on the task at hand, praying that the man making the drop would finally show up.

"Peter Duncan."

"Who's there?" he shouted, flailing his arms frantically as the ghostly voice echoed in the night. "That you Lincoln, you freakin' dirt bag? I told you to screw off."

When no answer came, Duncan knelt on the ground and placed his hands over his ears. "There's no one there. Stop listening to it. It's all in your stupid mind."

"Peter Duncan."

"It's not real," he insisted. "None of this is."

Duncan shrieked as he felt something grasp his ankles. His legs pulled out from under him, he fell face first to the pavement, his nose breaking as blood spurted everywhere. He felt himself being dragged into the abyss, his body limp as it slid across the harsh ground. Suddenly, he was tossed into the air, his neck snapping as he landed on his back with a thud. Looking up, he saw a figure shrouded in black hovering over him, the demon-like monster seething as it placed its powerful hands-on Duncan's sunken chest.

"Take this message back to your master," the vigilante growled, grabbing Duncan's left wrist, applying pressure to the man's elbow, and snapped it like a twig. Duncan tried to scream, but nothing came out of his lungs but a gasp of air. Duncan's right leg was yanked forward, an elbow crashing into the side of his knee, shattering his knee cap. "Tell him…I am the Black Plague."

Duncan's broken body fell silent, a heaving lump on the ground. The dark figure was gone, disappearing as quickly as he arrived. Seconds later a crimson red Cadillac pulled up, parking on Banks Avenue near where Duncan had stood just moments ago. Two men jumped out, grabbed the badly injured man and threw him into the car before speeding off.

As the taillights faded in the distance, Keith Lincoln came running around the corner, too late to catch a glimpse of the license plate. He looked around the area and found the trail of blood, capturing shots of the fresh crime scene on his cell phone. He punched Lieutenant Morgan's number in and waited for the cop to answer.

"Jesus, Mary and Charlie," Morgan shouted into the phone. "Do you have any idea what time it is, Skippy? If you got your ass arrested at the border again-"

"I saw him," Lincoln said, his old instincts kicking in as he surveyed the scene. "The guy in black, I saw him."

There was a pause on the other end of the phone. "You *are* piss ass drunk, aren't you?"

"Boss, get down to Banks and West 12th. Your guys should be pulling up in a second." Lincoln hung up as the first police cruisers arrived. The cops stepped out and looked past Lincoln toward a nearby brick, apartment building wall.

"Ho-ly shit," one of the cops said, pointing toward the wall. "What the hell is that?"

"What?" Lincoln said as he turned toward the wall. "Jesus Christ, what the hell?"

"Now I have witnessed what all of the whispers have been about. I know now, for a fact, that this is no late night ghost story. I saw him, not up-close but from a distance. What he did to some unfortunate, yet probably deserving soul was right out of a Batman storyline, like nothing I've ever witnessed before. But it was what I discovered once he had disappeared that was most frightening. Scrawled upon a nearby building, its intent unmistakable. 'I AM THE BLACK PLAGUE' He's announced his presence, no question, but what does this mean? Is Harbor City's vigilante tied more to the virus than we already imagined? The police did everything they could to block the media's view as they quickly covered the tag, but no whitewashing of the truth will change what I saw and soften the hell that I believe this city is about to endure once again." - BlueWave.com

11

The severely injured man howled in pain as he was carried through the back door of the Bistro, his maimed body callously dropped to the ground. He curled up into a fetal position, trembling from the agony running through him. He opened his eyes and saw a pair of candy apple red stilettos just inches away, peering up to see the beauty towering over him.

"Thank you, Ms. Bianchi," Duncan cried, tears streaming down his anguished face. "You saved my life."

"What did you see?" she asked, her voice lacking any sense of sympathy for the fallen underling. "Did you see him?"

"Yes," Duncan replied quickly, as his vision started to blur. "He was…a monster. All black. Red eyes, like the devil."

"So you didn't see his face?"

Duncan shook his head, as he felt a cold chill run through his body. "He has no face. It's just…black."

Erica began to pace, Franco and two other bodyguards stepping aside to make room for the fuming crime boss. She stayed quiet, trying to collect her thoughts and plan her next move. This was the first true challenge she had faced since assuming the throne vacated by her father's death. She knew how Alfonse Bianchi would have handled one of his foes. However, facing a nameless, faceless threat complicated her response.

"He said to give you a message," Duncan said, his teeth chattering as his body began to slip into shock. "He called himself Black Plague. Something strange like that."

Erica stopped pacing, glaring down at the man. "He said that?"

"Yes, the Black Plague. He said to tell you that."

Erica fumed, fire in her eyes. The muscles in her toned arms and legs tightened, her jaw locking in place. Her bodyguards stepped back, sensing an imminent eruption from their irascible boss. She composed herself, kneeling down to where Duncan lie shivering.

"You did well tonight. You did exactly what I asked of you."

Duncan was confused. "But, I-"

"I sent you out there for a reason," Erica said, her bright red lips forming a sly, seductive smile. "It wasn't for a pickup. There was no pickup. I needed you to face this evil that threatens what we have, that threatens our thing. You did that tonight. Well done."

Duncan looked the woman dead in the eye. "You…you used me for bait?"

Erica's smile grew broader, as she leaned forward and kissed the man's ice-cold forehead. She stood and placed her right hand out, Franco quickly handing her a .38 revolver from his waistband. She pointed it at Duncan's head and pulled the trigger three times.

"Throw him in the Harbor, with dignity," she ordered the men. "He was a good soldier. He deserves that much."

###

Charles Winston stood silently and still, once again peering out his penthouse window toward the grand lighthouse as the sun rose over Harbor City. He felt the presence in the room of his disciple, the unstoppable force emitting a power far greater than Charles had even anticipated. Ernest knew there was no need to announce the man's entry into the room, for his boss had a sixth sense that was quite indescribable.

"You know last night was a setup, correct?" Winston asked rhetorically.

"Not sure what you mean by that," the Black Plague vigilante said as he leaned back into the Italian leather sofa next to the bar. "Who got set up?"

"You did. Well, rather, we did. She wants to find out who you are, what you are, so she sacrificed one of her own. No loss to her, the subject was small time, at best."

"She?" he asked. "Who's she?"

Winston left the window and took a seat in his chair behind his desk. "She, my friend, controls all organized crime in our city. Erica Bianchi, daughter of Alfonse. Far more dangerous than her father ever was. She's new blood, no traditional mob codes to follow anymore. She's unpredictable, emotional, and highly skilled at what she does."

"You're telling me an old world mobster like Alfonse Bianchi turned over Harbor City to his daughter? I'm not buying that. As long as the old man's alive-"

"He's not," Winston interrupted. "And she took the torch not through entitlement, but by force. Tells you all you need to know."

The man sat quietly for a moment, retracing his steps from his assault on Peter Duncan just hours earlier. "Okay, so this is what we wanted anyway, right? To send a message to the politicians and the mob, whoever's running things. Makes no difference if it's Alfonse, his daughter or Jack the Ripper. We've made our statement, and nothing changes, right?"

"The only thing that changes now is that they have a target. You are no longer this invisible, mythical creature stalking the night. You've announced yourself to her, to the entire city with your branding."

"That was a nice touch, wasn't it?"

"When the city wakes up this morning the media will introduce them to the Black Plague," Winston said, more pride than trepidation in his voice. "Some will welcome your arrival; the good, honest people we have left here. But there will be those who won't be as thrilled. The scum, the politicians who enabled the scum to breed…"

"McSorley."

"Among others. The police will have their feathers ruffled. Lord knows they don't enjoy light being shone on their incompetence."

"And then there's Erica Bianchi, right?"

Winston cleared his throat. "I'm afraid it is whom Erica has become which is the real threat to all of us. She is as formidable a figure as Harbor City has ever seen. I'm sure she will be introducing herself to you soon enough, so be prepared. Extremely prepared."

12

Lieutenant Morgan arrived at Police Headquarters at nine fifteen on a hot, humid morning, already late for his meeting with the Police Commissioner. This was only the second time in his career he had been summoned to the 'big office,' the first coming in the latter days of the virus when crime first began to skyrocket, and the beleaguered investigator found himself struggling to close cases and deliver any positive results with a staff decimated by illness. That meeting was more of a loud, combative argument, as the city's top cop demanded arrests while its detective commander pointed his finger directly at City Hall. Any hope that the commissioner would go easy on the lieutenant were dashed that day, even though he had worked alongside her father a decade earlier.

Morgan exited the elevator on the seventh floor and walked briskly along the red carpet to a desk where a young female officer sat. She smiled and nodded, phoned the commissioner, and escorted him toward the office.

Kathleen Belanger was a blue-blooded, tough Harbor City cop. An Army vet, Belanger's grandfather, Earl, served nearly thirty years on the street, while her father Mark rose to the rank of captain before retiring after seeing his daughter get promoted to sergeant fifteen years ago. She had to overcome many obstacles during her career, from sexism and racism from the deeply inbred old boys club, to cries of nepotism as she climbed the professional ladder. However, beyond the usual and expected criticism from some male counterparts, there wasn't a cop on the job that wouldn't take Belanger as a partner. She was all business, no-nonsense and could hold her own against any of the street's thugs. She abided by the code of having each other's back no matter what, preferring to deal with issues inside precinct walls as opposed to airing dirty laundry for the frenzied media to pick apart.

Now entering her second year as commissioner, Belanger was still trying to steady the sinking ship that was the Harbor City PD. The fallout from the virus still hung over the troubled agency, and she was doing her best to restore morale to the rank and file as well as the citizenry. The last thing needed was an out of control vigilante.

"We have a serious problem," the Commissioner said before Morgan could make himself comfortable in the chair across from her. "Give me some good news."

Morgan looked toward the office ceiling, searching his brain for even a sliver of hopeful information. "Well, the good news is, whoever this person is, he's only targeting a select group of douchebags. Oh, I'm sorry, commissioner. Can I say douchebags?"

Belanger glared at Morgan, clearly not the slightest bit amused.

"Okay, I guess not. That's why I usually call them stink bugs, to avoid awkward looks. Anyway, everyone that's been hit by this guy has been an ex-con, each one of them paroled by the Mayor a couple of years ago. The first four DOAs were, as you know, the fab four that killed Anna Winston and walked away free as an ostrich. That's on DA Flagg's hands. The last two assault victims are low level thugs tied to the Bianchi's. I'm told there was a third, but that hasn't been confirmed. Look, he's got an agenda. These people are cockroaches, Commissioner. Shit bags, all of them. It's not like he's running around town taking out nurses and Peace Corps volunteers."

Belanger's glare grew more intense.

"Damn, I said shit bags, right? I meant stink bugs. Permission to speak freely?"

"Denied." Belanger snapped.

"I figured."

Belanger rose from behind her desk and began to pace her office. "I was told about the tag at the crime scene. The Black Plague. I ordered it removed immediately. The last thing we need is that popping up on the front pages. What do you think it means? What are we looking at next? A chemical attack of some sort? Biological?"

Morgan shook his head. "Damned if I know."

Belanger was starting to lose her patience. "Lieutenant, my father has always spoke well of you. That has earned you at least the benefit of the doubt so far. But right now, you're about one minute away from walking a midnight foot post at St. John's Cemetery for the last few weeks of your career."

"Commissioner, I ain't bullshittin' you. My detectives have nothing. No witnesses, no DNA, not a goddam hair from his ass. I'm gonna be leaning on a guy who knows the streets, knows the players, knows the game. He's our best bet right now."

Belanger took a seat on the edge of her desk and crossed her legs. "Please don't tell me it's Lincoln. He and his irresponsible website-"

"He knows the game, commissioner."

"He's a degenerate alcoholic, Lieutenant, and the botched Winston case remains a stain on this Department. He crossed the line. The so-called inside information he posts are the rants of a seriously disturbed individual. A bitter man. He's not who I want being the focal point of an investigation in my department."

"You're right." Morgan said.

"So you agree?"

"You're right about the degenerate alcoholic part, and the disturbed individual stuff. Guy is seriously screwed up, and a walking social disease. But I think he's our best play right now. He can get close to people we can't, and if our vigilante is a cop, my boy Lincoln will hear the whispers."

Belanger studied Morgan for several awkward seconds, weighing her options. "Lieutenant, let me let you in on something that normally is well above your pay grade. Next week, Mayor McSorley is going to officially announce he's running for re-election. The announcement will take place at a black tie, two thousand dollar-a plate fundraiser at the William J. Murray Museum. Now, I really don't have to explain how embarrassing it would be to City Hall if this vigilante nonsense is plastered all over the media right now?"

"Nope, no need to expatiate."

"Do you even know what that word means?" Belanger asked.

Morgan stood and bowed before the Commissioner, his sarcastic gesture again annoying the top cop. The lieutenant walked briskly out of her office without another word spoken between the two and took the elevator down to street level. Waiting for him outside, leaning on a dirty old mailbox, was Keith Lincoln.

"So, how'd that go?" he asked.

"Like we expected, Skippy. A goddam shit show," Morgan answered as the two men began the three block walk down to Pippen's Diner on East 14th Street. "I mentioned your name and she almost lost her breakfast."

The two men arrived at the diner and took their usual seat in a corner booth near the kitchen. Morgan ordered two eggs with cheese on a roll, while Lincoln asked the red headed waitress for a pot of coffee.

"Long night?" Morgan asked.

"Any other kinds?"

Morgan laughed, before his mood quickly turned serious. "Listen, we need to find this crazy bastard now. McSorley's gonna start campaigning for re-election next week."

"Wonderful news."

"Big announcement at some huge dollar shindig at the Murray Museum. Belanger made it clear, this shit blows up, I'm gonna get hung by my balls with the words 'retired old fool' stamped on my ass. So, whoever you've been shaking down for info, you need to turn up the heat, my friend. You got any gut feels yet?"

"Two things. One, if it is a cop, it has to be Tommy Wilson. He's got the background, the temper and the martial arts crap. He's capable, no doubt. Secondly, the car that got Duncan away from the crime scene, that had to be Erica Bianchi's men. So, we know the mob's gonna be coming hard after this guy real soon."

Morgan wiped the egg off his mouth and took a swig of orange juice. "How do you know about Erica Bianchi? I didn't tell you that."

"Got it from someone else." Lincoln said. "You're not my only source. Third, and this might be out of left field, but do you remember Mickey Moran?"

"Moran, from Chicago? He was the muscle for the Amonte family, before he went full blown rat and testified against Benito. He's deep in witness protection, isn't he?"

"He turned it down, told the feds to kiss his ass." Lincoln said, refreshing Morgan's memory. "Last I heard he's living in Arlington Heights, right under the mob's noses. If you remember, he laid some pretty bad beatings on anyone that crossed the Amonte's, including his own brother."

"Yeah, I remember. He beat that kid-touching pedophile to death on Lake Shore Drive a few years ago. Jury wanted to give him a medal instead of a conviction. Everybody did. Bad dude with a streak of morality. Fits the profile, I guess."

"Again, it's a long shot, but street justice was his calling card. Maybe he's looking to return to that life, move in on the Mafia Princess' turf and go to war with Chicago."

"Jesus, that's a stretch but…. it's a play. Let's pay him a visit, right after you go talk to the princess."

Lincoln nearly spit out his coffee. "What? Me?"

"I got nowhere with her, and no other cop can get close. But you might be able to. Just use that broken down, homeless guy charm of yours. How could any woman resist?"

"You want me to just walk into her place-"

"Walk, skip, jump, do a friggin' somersault for all I care," Morgan said as he tossed a twenty-dollar bill onto the table. "I just need you two to put your dumbass heads together and get this clown off the streets. If it's Wilson, you let me know and I'll take him down. If not, Arlington Heights is only two hours away."

Lincoln fiddled with the twenty as Morgan headed for the door. "You know there's a good chance she kills me right then and there, if I can even get near her."

Morgan stopped and looked back. "A very good chance, so make sure you change your socks and wash your ass. Make a good impression on the woman, Lincoln. You smell like a dead hooker."

Lincoln lifted both arms, checking his scent as Morgan left quickly. Meeting with Bianchi or even Moran was not something he envisioned, but it made sense. Not only would it keep Morgan chasing his tail, buying himself more time, but it might slow down the inevitable mob firestorm he knew was headed his way. His acting skills were about to be severely tested. However, first there was the matter of Tommy Wilson.

13

"Sector David, respond to a 10-52 family dispute. 1077 Michigan Avenue. Private house. Husband assaulting wife."

Tommy Wilson hit the lights as Linda Esperanza grabbed her radio and acknowledged the call. The cruiser flew through the west side, avoiding midday traffic as they closed in on what had become a chronic location for the police. Angelo Sanchez, a local mechanic, alcoholic and womanizer, had become increasingly violent with his wife Olivia over the past several weeks, dodging the cops on at least four prior occasions where she had called 911 fearing for her life. Each time, Angelo would return home, sobered up with flowers in hand, and his wife of eight years would welcome him back under the condition he stop drinking. Each attempt failed miserably.

The police cruiser screeched to a halt in front of the address. Wilson and Esperanza headed to the front door and announced their arrival. Olivia, a petite brunette of Columbian descent, answered the door "Jesus, Olivia," Linda said as she examined the woman's bruised face. "How many more times are you going to let him do this to you?"

"I thought he did it," the woman said. "I thought he gave it up this time. He was doing well, no beer in the fridge for a few days. Then last night-"

"Let me guess," Wilson interrupted. "He stayed out all night, came home this morning smelling like someone else's perfume, you called him on it, and he smacked you around. Same story as last time, Olivia, and the time before, and-"

"Okay, Tommy," Linda snapped, before turning back to the wife. "Where is he right now?"

Olivia shrugged her shoulders. "I really don't know."

"Stop protecting this piece of crap," Wilson said angrily. "Every time we come here you have no idea where he is. You keep lying for him and one day he's gonna slit your throat."

"I swear!" Olivia shouted as she started crying. "I don't know where he goes. Somewhere to blow off steam, to calm himself down-"

"To screw around with one of his side pieces, that's where," Wilson replied. "Take a report, Linda. I'll wait out here. I can't listen to this anymore."

Linda shot her partner an angry look before stepping inside the home. Wilson walked back to the car and leaned on the hood, crossing his arms and looking up at the blazing summer sun. A few seconds later he heard footsteps approaching from his left. He squinted and rubbed the sunlight out of his eyes, immediately recognizing the tall, thin male with the salt and pepper goatee.

"Well, well, well. Angelo, long time no see," Wilson said as he walked toward the man.

"What are you guys doing here?" Angelo Sanchez asked. "Everything ok?"

"You tell me," Wilson said. "Problems with the wife again, Angelo? Too much to drink? Treating her like a goddam punching bag, you sunavabitch?"

Angelo put his hands up in surrender. "I…I don't know what you're talking about. I didn't touch her."

Wilson's anger was growing by the second. He advanced on the man as Angelo slowly backed away. "Why don't you raise your hands to me, tough guy?"

"I don't want no problems with you," Angelo said, back peddling. "I didn't touch her. She's a lying bitch."

Wilson snapped. He reached out and grabbed the man by the throat, Angelo squealing as he struggled for air. Wilson then placed his large hands over the man's face and shoved him backwards, sending Angelo sprawling into a set of nearby garbage cans.

"Get up, you piece of shit," Wilson said as he removed his handcuffs from his belt. "You like hitting women? Let's see how tough you are now."

Angelo crawled out from under the garbage strewn over him and begged Wilson to stop. The cop grabbed him by his hair, tossed him onto the back of the car and cuffed him as the suspect wailed in pain. "You're lucky I don't break you in half right here."

Angelo cried out to his wife as Wilson threw him into the backseat of the car. The cop grabbed his radio and informed his partner of the arrest and waited for Linda to come out of the house. While he waited, he saw a crowd forming across the street, several neighborhood residents filming the cop's actions on their cell phone cameras. Wilson scowled at the group, before recognizing one man near the adjacent corner.

"What the hell are you doing here?" Wilson asked as he headed over to confront the man.

Keith Lincoln raised the paper bag to his mouth and took a sip of beer from the can inside. "Not much. Just taking a walk on a nice day, saw the crowd and was wondering what's going on. How's your day going, Tommy?"

"Bullshit," Wilson barked. "You're a goddam liar, and you suck at it too."

"No, I'm serious," Lincoln replied. "I saw you rolling with that guy. Thought I'd hang around to see if you needed help. I got your back, big guy."

Wilson's face reddened with anger. "You're following me?"

"What? No, of course not," Lincoln laughed. "Why would I do such a thing? You're really not that interesting."

"Cause you don't have shit on this vigilante story and you want to try and pin it on me. You're still pissed that I busted your nose, but you're not man enough to do anything about it."

Lincoln took another sip of his beer and shook his head. "You're way off, Tommy, but I gotta tell you, you took down that little guy easily. Still got those mad karate skills. Pretty impressive, grasshopper.”

“Screw off, Lincoln,” Wilson said as he headed back to his patrol car. “You think I'm the vigilante, go ahead and prove it. But we all know who it really is, don't we?”

“Maybe,” Lincoln said. “We'll find out, I guess.”

14

The William J. Murray Museum was filled with the rich and powerful; billionaire financiers, entrepreneurs, politicians and celebrities from Chicago rubbing elbows and comparing stock portfolios with the locals. Each had a stake in any semblance of a Harbor City revival, as outside investors looked to prey upon a city mired in fear and apathy. The only homegrown figure who could hold a candle to the Windy City's elite arrived shortly after eight, fashionably late and with his chauffeur by his side.

Charles Winston looked upon the crowd with disdain. For decades Chicago elitists downplayed his wealth, looking down upon his fortune as borne from a second-class city. He hid his anger well, putting aside his resentment in order to stay connected to the power circles across the country. He was aware those that were in attendance on this evening were nothing more than vultures picking off a long dead carcass, hoping they could claim a piece of an improbable resurrection.

"Charlie Winston, how the hell are you?" asked Chicago Mayor Ralph Paone, a stocky, grey haired, cigar chomping figure right out of central casting. "Some night, huh? You got everybody here. Michael Jordan's over there by the band, Butkus and Ditka are at table three. Is that Johnny Bench over by the fruit cup?"

Winston could barely feign interest. "There are people here who are far more important than athletes, Ralph."

"Who, the politicians?" Ralph belly laughed. "You know I despise those stuffed shirts. I've never been one of them, that's why my people love me. Hey, is that Bruce Springsteen over there?"

Relieved that the star gazing Chicago mayor ran off, Winston made eye contact with Ernest and the two men headed for their seats at table one.

A long, black limousine escorted by two dark SUVs arrived near the museum's rear loading dock. Mayor Marty McSorley emerged, followed by his wife Sonja and their seven-detective security detail. They slid in quietly, cutting through the kitchen to avoid the throngs of well-wishers and hangers-on. McSorley was never quite the people person, his anti-social behaviors somehow overlooked by Harbor City's voters who instead concentrated on his left-leaning agenda to elect him in a landslide. Capturing a second term was going to be a far greater challenge for the socially awkward Chicago native, which is why he hired some of the top public relations and speech writers in the country as his campaign was about to commence.

McSorley had been given the nickname 'Big Bird' by his detractors, alluding to his frame and protruding nose that resembled the famous children's character. His eventual opponents would undoubtedly pin the derogatory name to him during the campaign, right alongside his early prison releases and failed pandemic lockdown policies.

The crowd of two hundred settled into their seats and began sipping on Dom Perignon and nibbling on their shrimp Caesar Salads. As the clock struck nine, Mayor McSorley entered the ballroom to thunderous applause and stood behind a podium with Sonja at his side. The ovation lasted nearly a minute as the sycophantic attendees made sure the Mayor felt their love.

"Thank you all so much," McSorley said as the crowd quieted and sat down. "What a wonderful summer night, right? If you go to the top of the Harbor Lighthouse you can see forever, and it's that glorious vision that has inspired me to continue to move this great city forward."

More applause came from the crowd, as Charles and Ernest sat expressionless at their table. Their indifference did not go unnoticed by Ralph Paone, now seated to the men's left.

"Loosen up Charlie, for chrissakes," the Mayor of Chicago said, his words slurred by an overindulgence at the open bar. "Holy crap, is that Harrison Ford at table seven?"

"Harbor City is undergoing an incredible revitalization as we speak," McSorley continued, many eyes in the crowd rolling as he laid out his perspective. "Just three years ago we were struck by an invisible enemy, a virus that took lives and destroyed our economy. Some predicted the death of our beloved city, but with decisive action we were able to stem the tide and survive. The rumors of our death have been greatly exaggerated. Harbor City is still standing, and my administration is responsible not only for its survival, but its rebirth!"

Charles cringed at McSorley's perverted view of himself and the city he destroyed. His distaste for the words spewing from the mayor's mouth evidenced by the sickly look on his face.

"Charlie, you need more booze," Paone laughed as he motioned toward Ernest. "Even your date looks like he's having more fun than you. Live it up a little."

Ernest held his tongue, instead envisioning himself snapping the round-bodied man's neck. Charles ignored the drunken rants, turning his attention back to McSorley's warped vision.

"With Harbor City on the rise, we simply can't afford to change course and revert to failed policies of previous administrations. With my beautiful wife by my side, we will ride our success to reelection and securing our city's return to greatness!"

The mention of McSorley's wife dug deep inside Charles. He glanced toward Ernest, who understood his boss' anger.

"I'd like to take this opportunity to present a quick look at our great city, how far we've come, and what lies ahead," McSorley said proudly. "My campaign production manager Kim and I put together a video I'm sure all of you will love. Can we show that now, please?"

On cue, the lights went down, and a beam of light shot across the room above McSorley's head. Soft Frank Sinatra music began to play as the video began with images of Harbor City at work and play.

"Our police officers, firefighters, paramedics, health care workers, teachers, all of those that helped pull us through the evil pandemic," McSorley narrated as images of the city's first responders and essential workers lit up the room. "Our children playing in the streets, innocents enjoying city life as they should."

Images of young mothers pushing baby carriages and strollers appeared, followed by those of senior citizens enjoying the sun on park benches. "The circle of life, playing out everywhere across Harbor City. A place where families can grow and build each day."

Suddenly, the video skipped and paused. The screen went black, before the word 'CRIME' appeared in bold, blood-red letters.

"Not sure why that's there," McSorley said, confused at the unexpected image. Still, the consummate politician recovered. "Well, my administration has driven crime to historic lows through education and tolerance as opposed to mass incarceration. Over-policing has no home here in Harbor City!"

The crowd applauded, before the word 'DRUGS' appeared, the guests suddenly looking at one another with confused glances.

"Drugs, yes of course," McSorley said, trying to hide his annoyance. "We are ridding our streets of dangerous drugs each and every day."

'MURDER'

"Mur…murder. Yes, murder," the mayor stuttered as he glared at the image which was also clearly not part of the production rehearsal Kim had presented earlier in the day. "Murder and other violent crimes are decreasing because we are rehabilitating offenders…"

'APATHY'

McSorley looked at his wife, who was equally bewildered by what was taking place. "We've eliminated apathy," he improvised. "Replaced it with hope; hope of a brighter future."

As two detectives raced toward a back room from where the feed was originating, Paone placed his empty champagne glass down and looked at Charles. "Am I totally plastered, or is somebody screwing with this guy?"

"RAPE'

"Ladies and gentlemen, I sincerely apologize," McSorley said sheepishly, unable to continue the weak charade. "Obviously we are having technical difficulties. Apparently, we've been hacked. Kim, can you hear me back there?"

The crowd gasped as an image of McSorley and his wife appeared on-screen, the word 'CRIMINALS' underneath.

"Whoever is responsible for this disgusting act of sabotage will be arrested and prosecuted to the fullest extent of the law!" the mayor roared, the crowd silent.

One of the detectives returned and whispered into the Mayor's ear, informing him that Kim was nowhere to be found. Several guests stood and began to leave, the strange events causing the elitists discomfort.

'THE BIG LIE' appeared next.

"What the hell?" McSorley raged. "Turn this goddam thing off!"

Another message appeared.

'FORCED VACCINATIONS. OLIVER INDUSTRIES. FOLLOW THE MONEY.'

Charles Winston smiled for the first time that evening.

'RYAN SAMBERG. CEO OF OLIVER INDUSTRIES. BROTHER OF SONJA MCSORLEY.'

"Lies!" McSorley shouted. "All lies!"

One final message appeared:

'THE BLACK PLAGUE.'

A sweat drenched McSorley grabbed his wife's hand and stormed away, heading for the kitchen door and the safety of their security team. As they entered, they found five of their detectives lying unconscious, badly beaten and disarmed. Next to them lie Kim, wincing in pain and completely disoriented.

"Jesus Christ," McSorley said, fear running through his body. He pulled his wife close as the kitchen lights went out, covering the couple in darkness. "Who's there? What the hell do you want?"

A whispering voice moved quietly through the kitchen.

"Your surrender, Mr. Mayor."

15

There was a flash of white light and a sudden sharp pain in the back of his head before everything went dark. When he opened his eyes, he found himself staring at a pair of black stilettos attached to the sexiest, finely toned legs he had ever seen. Looking up, he saw the striking woman glaring down at him.

"What the hell hit me?" Keith Lincoln said as he rose to his knees, his head throbbing.

"Franco," Erica Bianchi replied. "He should have killed you, but I would really like to find out why a disgrace of a cop has been asking questions about me. You want to talk, Mr. Lincoln, you have thirty seconds of my time."

Lincoln tried to clear his rattled brain as he remained bowed at the woman's feet. "Ms. Bianchi, I come to you with all due…"

"Mr. Lincoln, you can lose the old-world lingo and drop the dramatics. My father is dead and so are many of his traditions and values. You now have less than twenty seconds."

Lincoln coughed into his hand, a trickle of blood running from his nose toward his upper lip. "I'm here to ask you if you'd like to help me find whoever is doing this to your people before a civilian gets caught in the middle."

Erica smirked. "Morgan sent you. Of course. Why the hell would I want or need your help? Look at you, you're a broken-down has-been, and your time is up. I expected more. Franco, see Mr. Lincoln out."

"That was definitely not twenty seconds," Lincoln said as Franco lifted him to his feet. "Look, the cops are trying to avert a blood bath in the streets. I know you won't work with them, but I have informants everywhere, inside and outside the department. You know that. That's how I ended up here."

Erica walked closer to where Franco held Lincoln by his shoulder. "I still don't see why I need help finding whoever this man is, unless he's a cop and they are protecting him. Perhaps you're protecting him, or maybe…"

"No, I'm not the vigilante, and that's exactly why you need me. You don't have one clue about this guy, do you?

Neither do the cops. But I'm getting closer. This guy, he knows your people and he can smell a cop in a heartbeat. But me, the street people I talk to, even you don't have those connections. People contact me through my website all the time, giving me info and tips they would never give the cops."

Erica turned and walked away from him, shaking her head in disbelief. "You haven't made a strong enough case, Mr. Lincoln. In fact, I think you're feeding me a lot of bullshit. Websites mean nothing. So you have a few big-mouth cops and losers on the street who slide you information that does absolutely nothing. You're out of your league. Goodbye, Mr. Lincoln."

Lincoln threw up a prayer. "What about Mickey Moran?"

The name caused Erica's expression to quickly morph from disinterest to anger. "What about that coward?"

"Look, I know your father and the Amonte family in Chicago had a truce in place, but Moran has no loyalty to anyone anymore. Beating people to death was his MO, especially those who crossed his twisted line of morality. He might be-"

"Moran, like most rodents, has no spine, Mr. Lincoln. But if he is behind this and has Harbor City in his sights, his demise will be swift and violent. I do thank you for the tip, though. Maybe you're not totally useless after all."

"Trust me, I'm not," he said as Franco tightened his grip. "And what happened at the museum tonight changes everything."

Erica looked inquisitively at the man. "Someone embarrassed the mayor. So what? He does that to himself on a daily basis. Changes nothing."

"What they're not telling you is this guy took out the mayor's entire security detail, tied up him and his wife and left them there for the press to see. The cops kept them away, but somebody there got cell phone video. They're scrambling to find whoever it was, but it's gonna hit the media big time, and that changes everything."

"Really? I don't see how."

Lincoln laughed. "Ok, I'll spell it out. After tonight the cops are going to go after him hard, and they'll want to get him before you do so they're not embarrassed. When they collar him and he goes away, he'll boast in prison how he took out six members of the Bianchi crime family and you couldn't touch him. He'll be a hero, run the prison yard. Maybe you can get to him in there, maybe not. That's a tough gamble with your reputation, Ms. Bianchi. Chicago will see it as weakness. How long before the Amonte's move on you then?"

Erica's anger grew as she listened to the man ramble on. "Weak, Mr. Lincoln? We'll see. Franco, bring Vincent in here, please."

Franco left the room, leaving Lincoln and Erica face to face again.

"I will show you how weak I am, Mr. Lincoln. Make sure you let your street people know and pass it on to Chicago as well."

"I didn't say you were weak, I said perception would be…"

Franco returned with Vincent LaTorre, an underling who ran Harbor City's most popular waterfront strip club. Lincoln and LaTorre had crossed paths several years ago during a buy and bust operation near the club, the latter ending up in handcuffs before the charges were later dropped.

"Well, well. Detective Lincoln," LaTorre said with a smirk. "I thought you were dead?"

"I get that a lot, Vinny." Lincoln replied.

"I'm sorry, Ms. Bianchi. You wanted to see me?" Vincent asked, turning his attention to the boss.

"Yes, I did. Vincent. I was going to hold off on this conversation but now seems to be the right time. I'm told your envelope was short this month. Any reason why?"

Vincent's eyes began to dart back and forth nervously. "It was less than a grand, Ms. Bianchi, and I told Franco that my mother's back in the hospital and her insurance doesn't cover the tests she's getting. Looks like her skin cancer came back. I told Franco I'd repay it next week. I swear. Tell her, Franco."

Franco shook his head. "I don't recall that conversation, Vinny."

"Franco," LaTorre pleaded. "Come on, what are you talkin' about? I told you-"

"There are no loans, Vincent. You know that." Erica suddenly whipped her right leg around and landed a devastating roundhouse kick to the right side of the man's head, sending him flying across the room. Lincoln stood in shock, having never seen such speed and power in a woman before. Franco grabbed Vincent and dragged him over to a nearby table, placing the man's right arm upon it.

"You steal from me, there are consequences," Erica said as she walked over and removed a silver machete from a corner closet. "The hands that take from their own can never be trusted again."

Vincent cried and pleaded with his boss as Franco held his arm down on the table. He begged Erica to stop, asking for forgiveness if he could repay the money by nightfall. Erica wore a blank expression on her face as she admired the shiny blade.

"You don't want to do this," Lincoln said, feeling obligated to speak up. "If what I said caused this-"

Erica raised the machete above her head and slammed it down, Vincent's limp, severed hand falling to the floor as he shrieked and fell unconscious.

"Point made," Lincoln said.

"I will find this coward and I will cut off far more than his hands," Erica said as she lay the bloody machete down and walked away. "Goodbye, Mr. Lincoln. You were quite disappointing."

Lincoln looked over at Franco. "Not the first time I've heard that from a woman."

"What I have feared most since this madness began is slowly becoming a reality. Law Enforcement and Organized Crime both want the vigilante's head on a platter. Attempts by both cops and yours truly to try and avoid a deadly scenario have fallen on deaf ears. So now, in light of the 'attack' on Mayor McSorley and his wife and the media about to blow the lid off of this, the clock is ticking to see who can grab this self-proclaimed 'Plague' first. We can only hope no one gets caught in the crossfire."

Keep your heads on a swivel, Harbor City. War is upon us.

-BlueWave.com

The modest colonial home sat quietly within Arlington Heights Village, a suburb which was home to just under eighty thousand residents who enjoyed living outside the fray of Chicago and Harbor City. Inhabited by primarily blue-collar city workers and retirees who kept to themselves in the upper-middle class neighborhood, the Village was also home to a reclusive figure who spent his days and nights on his wraparound porch, sipping screwdrivers and indulging in his favorite pastime. Neighbors walking past the two-hundred-year-old home would smile and wave at the man out of habit, reciprocation rare if at all.

Lieutenant Morgan walked up to the three-foot-high gate that surrounded 2130 Belfour Drive and made eye contact with the man, who struggled to recognize the face looking back at him. After a few moments, a quizzical look came across the weathered features of one of the most feared and loathed mob figures in the history of the Midwest.

"Where do I know you from?" asked Mickey Moran, leaning forward in his antique rocking chair.

"Didn't we go to Harvard together?" Morgan replied, his sarcasm eliciting a grin from the former mob strongman.

"Nah, can't be," Moran countered. "I'm a Yale man myself."

Morgan climbed the three steps up to the porch and sat down on a rickety wooden bench across from Moran. He checked his watch, cursing Lincoln under his breath for being late. "We got a problem over in Harbor City, Mickey. I know you've still got connections, those inside that are somehow still loyal to you, even after what you did."

Moran rocked slowly in his chair, measuring his response carefully. "I may hear things, but I'm not involved anymore. I'm living a clean and quiet life. Erica Bianchi's your problem, not mine. She's not her father. She's got no business sense. All blood and violence. I abhor violence, for the record."

"Since when did you start abhorring?" Morgan chided him. "After the twentieth dude you beat senseless for the Amonte's?"

"Not sure what you're talking about. I've never been convicted of jaywalking, never mind anything to do with people getting hurt."

"Of course not," Morgan shot back. "You made a deal and rolled over on Benito Amonte faster than one of those Pillsbury croissant things. You saved your hide. I'm amazed they haven't put one in the back of your dopey head yet, especially with you sittin' out here in the open daring them to."

Moran laughed and waved dismissively at Morgan. "Come on, stop reading those trash newspapers. They fill your head with negative thoughts. Now, if you've got nothing else to say-"

"The vigilante. The Black Plague. Hear anything about that?"

Moran frowned. "Why would I? Again, that's your problem."

Morgan again checked his watch, looking around for any sign of Lincoln. "Somebody beating the pulp out of low-level stink bugs, moving in on Bianchi territory after Alfonse keeled over. I'm just figurin' someone like you might see an opportunity to stick it to Chicago one more time."

"You think I'm the vigilante? Oh, that's funny. You Harbor City boys really are grasping for straws, aren't you? You can't see the old billionaire is pulling the strings there? He hired some mercenary to off the mutts that killed his wife and now he's going after your idiot Mayor to even some political score. There you go, I just closed the case for you. You're welcome."

Morgan shook his head. "Okay, so who's the mercenary? Hear anything about that?"

Moran hesitated, a wide grin slowly spreading across his face. "I might have. Come inside, I'll make some green tea. Like lemon with that?"

"Green tea?" Morgan asked as he stood and followed Moran inside. "Dammit, fool, did you surrender your testicles in that deal with the feds?"

Moran led the lieutenant into the modest, white-walled kitchen and placed a pot of water on the stove as Morgan sat at the oak table nearby. "It has antioxidants. Keeps arthritis away."

"That's amazing information," Morgan said, once again without the slightest attempt to hide his sarcasm. "Now, talk to me. Who's the vigilante?"

Moran looked over at the lieutenant with astonishment. "Seriously, you really don't have a clue, do you?"

"If I did would I be sittin' here waiting for Mary Poppins to brew me a sissy-ass tea and draw me a friggin' bath!" Morgan snapped. "Spit it out, meathead."

"Okay, okay. Calm down. Bad for your blood pressure. The guy you're looking for is right under your nose. How you missed it is the real question."

"So it is a cop, right?" Morgan asked. "Tommy Wilson?"

"Let me just say-" Suddenly, blood spurted from Moran's forehead onto Morgan's shirt. A bullet had crashed through the kitchen window and sliced through the former mob enforcer's skull. He stumbled forward and fell hard to the floor, killed instantly. Morgan was paralyzed for a split second, his brain trying to digest what had just happened in front of his eyes. Instinctively, he drew his weapon and dropped to the floor, rolling under the table for cover. He heard the unmistakable sound of wheels spinning and a car speeding away from the house.

"This is Lieutenant Morgan, Harbor City PD!" he shouted into his cell phone after dialing 911. "I need some cops and an ambulance over at 2130 Belfour! Male shot!"

The front door swung open, Lincoln rushing in to find Morgan crouched under the table and Moran lying in his own blood as sirens wailed in the distance. "Jesus Christ, I was walking up the street and I heard a shot. What the hell happened?"

Morgan climbed out and stuffed his gun back in his holster. "Karma is one cold hearted bitch."

16

"Let me commend you on a virtuoso performance."

Charles Winston beamed with pride as he placed his hands on the shoulders of the man known as The Black Plague. "You sent a very powerful message to the powerful themselves. I don't believe they feel as untouchable anymore."

Instead of being emboldened by the man's praise, the vigilante shook his head and looked down at his feet. "The museum was a success last night, but I may have cost someone their life this morning."

"Mickey Moran?" Winston asked. "Please. Live by the sword, die by the sword. Moran knew once he turned State's evidence this was an inevitability."

"Maybe," the vigilante said. "But I told Erica that he-"

"Enough regret. There is too much of that in this world. Keith Lincoln used Moran to throw the lieutenant and Erica off his trail and it worked brilliantly. Now, let's celebrate the downfall of the Mayor and the incredible work by you and

Ernest. His hacking of the presentation was quite impressive, I'm sure you agree."

"So what's next?" the man asked. "We've humiliated McSorley, as was your wish."

Winston lowered his hands and looked the man dead in the eye. "What's next, my dear warrior, is what we have truly prepared you for. The powers that be will exhaust all resources trying to capture and expose you. Erica and her minions will do the same, though the form of punishment they have planned will be far greater and much more excruciating. Now that you've seen her for what she is, up close and personal, you understand she has few limits. The skills with which Ernest has imparted upon you will be tested, as will your inner strength and ability to overcome what undoubtedly lies ahead. This is your time."

The man realized the gravity of the task at hand. He again looked toward the sky as if seeking strength from God and the heavens. He turned toward Ernest and approached him, seeking reinforcement from his mentor.

"Do you believe I'm ready?"

Ernest stayed silent. His steely gaze and locked jaw answered the man's question.

"In doubt, there is defeat, young man," Winston said. "You and you alone know if you are ready to endure this next phase."

The vigilante took a deep breath, expanding his chest and clearing his mind. "I am ready."

Winston smiled broadly again. "I knew you were. The Black Plague has just begun to rise."

He headed off into the night once again, inspired by faith yet frightened by fate. He made his way to the West Side under the cover of darkness, taking his position on a building fire escape off West 33rd Street. He waited for his prey, having studied the gun runner's routine for several nights. Once midnight struck, the man would arrive to consummate another deal. The Black Plague was in place and ready to strike, but a hollow feeling filled his body with a sense of dread he had not felt since undertaking this mission. His mind flashed back to his encounter with Erica, everything about her pure evil. He had been lying to the one person he trusted in the city in order to keep him off-balance. He lied each night to his loyal website followers, providing just enough information to keep them interested and the McSorley administration worried. He had surrendered all control of his life for a chance at revenge and redemption, but it all seemed to be spiraling out of control quickly.

"What the hell am I doing?"

###

Marty McSorley's scowl sent a clear message. Commissioner Belanger sat next to Lieutenant Morgan across from the mayor, each able to feel the heat emanating from the city's top official. Amateur cell phone video captured from the Murray Museum had leaked to the national media, showing a bound and humiliated Mayor and First Lady. The embarrassment regarding inept security was bad enough, the perception of complete government impotence far worse.

"I want to know how this happened," McSorley raged. "Some lunatic is running around my city like a psycho ninja and you let him attack me and my wife? Seven detectives on my security detail, thirty cops around the museum, and no one sees him? He humiliated me in front of the entire world!"

Belanger shifted in her seat, trying to come up with a valid reply. "Your honor, I apologize and take full responsibility. I felt the manpower was sufficient to stop-."

"You were wrong, Commissioner!" McSorley shouted as his head nearly exploded. "How could one man-"

"Your eminence," Morgan interrupted facetiously. "This psycho ninja, as you call him, has been kicking the living shit out of the perps you let walk free the last two years. Unless your head's been buried in the sand or up your keester, you had to expect the violence would escalate to a point where no one was safe, not even you."

"Lieutenant, I sincerely dislike you," McSorley growled. "Why are you even here? I don't recall-"

"He's in charge of the Vigilante Task Force I created a few weeks ago, sir."

Morgan shot Belanger a confused look. "I am?"

"Vigilante Task Force, huh?" McSorley said, his rage simmering. "How's that working out so far? Let's see, you went on a field trip to Chicago and wound up in the middle of a homicide, right Lieutenant?"

"Moran was assassinated by either the Bianchi's or the Amonte's for their own reasons. My business had nothing-"

"Nothing to do with it?" McSorley fumed. "I give up. The incompetence level is astounding."

Belanger cleared her throat. "Sir, we've made significant progress in the case. We feel we're closing in on a suspect and-"

"Enough!" McSorley snapped, silencing his top cop. He sat and smoldered for nearly half a minute, holding his head in his hands. "Let's cut through all the bullshit and lay it out there. Whoever this is works for Charlie Winston, correct?"

Belanger and Morgan exchanged glances before the Lieutenant spoke up. "Uh, we can't confirm or deny that just yet. There's a whole lotta people out there you pissed off and going over each and every one of them takes time."

"He's never forgiven me for his wife's death," McSorley sighed. "We've had disagreements before that were business-related, but he blames me for Anna. He's even angrier that those four young men weren't convicted, but we can't allow police misconduct and wrongful convictions. If he's angry with anyone it should be that dirty cop, Lincoln. Speaking of which, I want him questioned immediately."

"Who, Lincoln?" asked an incredulous Morgan. "You're way off base, Skippy."

"What did you just say?"

"Never mind."

"I know it was him who hacked our presentation, made me look like a fool. That website of his, spouting lies and garbage about me. Dragging my wife's family into it now. He's got motive. Bring him in and grill him till he confesses."

Morgan fought hard to hide his amusement. "Hot lights and sleep deprivation could work. If not, we could always water board his ass."

"Just do your job, Lieutenant," McSorley fumed.

Morgan nodded and jotted Winston's name down in his pad. "Charlie Winston and Keith Lincoln. If ever there were two dudes that didn't belong in the same room."

"Just do it," McSorley ordered. "I want this maniac in handcuffs before somebody else gets killed or maimed. Understood?"

"Understood, your honor," Belanger said. "In the meantime, we'll do our best to try and control the media, but I'd be prepared for this getting a lot worse before it gets better, to be totally honest."

McSorley grabbed the morning newspaper off his desk and held it up. The front-page headlines screamed 'BLACK PLAGUE VIGILANTE STRIKES AGAIN.' The accompanying photo was already social media fodder. "My wife and I, hogtied like goddam farm animals, this psycho taunting and spreading lies about us, and you're telling me it's gonna get worse?"

"Yeah, good point. Probably not." Morgan said, before the Mayor exploded again and ordered both Morgan and Belanger out of his office.

17

Abigail Miller Lincoln looked at the man standing in her doorway, her estranged husband looking as if he hadn't slept in years. It had been almost a year since she had last seen him, and she wasn't about to throw roses at the man's feet upon his surprise visit.

"Can I come in, Abby?" he asked sheepishly after several awkward seconds of staring at each other in silence.

Abigail said nothing, although her body language was defiant and unwelcoming. She relented, however, stepping aside to allow him into her modest, one-bedroom ranch home in the tiny Harbor City suburb of Santo Heights. The strawberry blonde woman wore the pain of the last two years on her face, her anguish aging her faster than Father Time himself. She led him into the living room and took a seat in her rocking chair as Keith Lincoln sat down on a sofa several feet away.

"Sorry I didn't call first," he said, his head bowed, and his eyes fixed on his worn, leather boots. "Didn't mean to catch you off guard."

"You haven't called me in months," Abigail said, her voice cracking. "I haven't seen your face in-"

"I know," Lincoln said, cutting her off. "It's not you. It's this house. It's just too much for me right now."

Abigail looked at the man she once loved with pity. "Because of me, or because of what you became?"

Lincoln took in a deep breath and exhaled the agony within him. He had fought hard to push away the heartbreak and mental noise that tormented him since he destroyed his marriage. He looked across at the woman seated in the rocking chair and could see she had been struggling mightily as well.

"I'm afraid I've become far worse now."

"Why are you here, Keith?" Abigail asked.

Lincoln clasped his hands together, trying to find an answer. "I'm not sure, Abby. Something's going on right now, and I think I've got myself in so deep I can't get out."

"You're gambling again?" she asked.

"No."

"Drinking?"

"Rarely, but just enough so people think I'm a fall-down drunk. Appearances sake."

"I don't understand?"

"Don't even try. Neither do I, sometimes."

"Please don't tell me you're doing drugs, Keith."

"No, never. You know me better than that, Abby."

Abigail wasn't sure she knew him at all. After ten years of marriage, she never envisioned their world falling apart, a union destroyed by an invisible intruder. "Is… it a woman?"

Lincoln shook his head. "No, Abby, it's not. The women come and go, but it's all a charade, again for appearances sake. A ridiculous act."

Abby shot him a perplexed look. "Who are you trying to fool?"

Lincoln laughed. "Everyone."

"I can't help you unless you tell me what's going on," Abby sighed. "You need to tell me."

Lincoln shook his head. "Not sure I can. This thing I've been doing, with the website. When I started it, I thought I was doing the right thing. Exposing corrupt politicians and the bullshit they pull on people, even their own cops. I thought I could do things with it that others couldn't. I could speak up for cops, tell their stories, let people know what was really going on behind the scenes and on the streets. But everything's changed now. Now I'm dealing with the worst kinds of people, dangerous people. The other night I found myself watching a mob boss…. it's gotten out of control, Abby. I crossed the line and I don't know how to go back."

"Jesus Christ, Keith," she gasped. "What the hell are you involved in?"

"I thought I knew, Abby. I thought it was right. I thought I can change everything that happened to me, everything that went wrong with us. Make everything right again. I was wrong. I feel worse. I've got blood on my hands that I can't just wash off."

Abigail looked into his eyes and realized her husband was not only lost, but truly frightened. "When the Department fired you, said you were a corrupt cop-"

"Abby please, don't go there."

"Keith, you'll never be able to live again unless you face it. You ran from it, and you left me behind to deal with it."

Lincoln's heart sank. The pain inside him was building again. Tears streamed down his face as his hands trembled. "They destroyed me, all for political gain. I didn't fight back, I didn't fight for us. I gave up, quit on everything, and thought I could bring them down with me with a stupid website and locker room rumors. This thing that I'm into now, I thought it would make the pain go away, by punishing them, all of them. But the pain's still there. Even as I've become someone else, something else, I still feel it and see it when I look in the mirror."

"Something else?"

"I've become a monster, Abby. Unstoppable, and uncontrollable."

Abigail saw the torture he was going through. There was a time she would have held her husband in her arms to console and comfort him. That time had passed. Now, there was only pity, confusion and anger. "Whatever it is you're doing will never give you your life back, the life we had together. It will only kill you in the end."

"I know it will," he said as he stood to leave, his legs wobbly. "Probably very soon.""You don't have to do it, Keith. You can walk away, start a new life. Start over again. We both can, but not if you're hell bent on killing yourself."

Lincoln wiped his cheek bones, the salt from his tears burning his eyes. Unsteady on his feet, he kissed Abby on the forehead and slinked away, shoulders hunched and heaving, leaving his ex-wife alone and crying, again. After twenty minutes of sobbing, she lifted herself out of her chair and shuffled to her den, taking a seat in front of her desktop computer and doing what she once considered the unthinkable. She pulled up BlueWave.com, the site she had sworn to never waste a second of her life on, and perused her husband's recent, cryptic ramblings about crime and the Harbor City vigilante. It was then, she knew.

"Oh my God, no."

18

Johnny Esplanade, a rugged gun dealer from Miami handpicked by Erica Bianchi to run her arms business up north, had not been seen on the street in close to a week. Each night, the Black Plague sat still in the night, waiting for Esplanade to appear and conduct his business. The sudden disappearing act worried him that Bianchi was changing her operation's routine to avoid the vigilante from interfering in her business. A sudden change of course would require him gathering more intelligence and information, which could take weeks or months, depending how frightened the street thugs were of either the new mob scion or the seemingly invisible vigilante.

It was nearly three a.m., two hours later than Esplanade's usual meet times. Just as the Plague was about to head home empty handed once again, a silver Dodge Charger roared down the street, parking at the dimly lit corner of West 33rd Street and Buckner Avenue. Two men exited the Dodge, one of them holding a black duffel bag. It was Esplanade, whom the vigilante recognized immediately by the three-inch scar on the left side of his face. The other man was Nicky Blackstone, a newcomer to the organized crime lifestyle still looking to make a name for himself in the Bianchi family on Esplanade's coattails.

As Esplanade and his cohort entered an alleyway between a closed bodega and a shuttered nail salon, the shadowy figure felt that uneasiness creep up inside of him again, a feeling he knew he would have to overcome to survive another encounter with Bianchi's men.

"What the hell am I doing?"

Esplanade and Blackstone stood side by side in the rear of the nail salon building, only a shred of moonlight illuminating the men. Twenty seconds later a black Cadillac Escalade arrived. Three young Hispanic men, each wearing black and silver bandanas, got out and headed down the alley. The Plague watched from above as the deal slowly unfolded.

One of the Hispanic men dropped a rolled-up paper bag at Esplanade's feet. Blackstone bent down and picked it up, showing the contents to his partner. There were several bundles of one-hundred-dollar bills. Esplanade smiled and placed the duffel bag on the ground, opened it, and revealed its contents; five high powered .45 caliber semi-automatic handguns, two hundred armor piercing rounds and four ballistic vests.

"So," Esplanade said. "We have a deal?"

As one of the Hispanic men stepped forward to retrieve the bag, they caught a glimpse of a dark figure blur past them. The five men pulled handguns out and twisted and turned in every direction looking for whatever had just buzzed them. Esplanade and Blacksmith backed off, fully aware of what was about to happen.

Almost immediately, the three Hispanics were under attack. The vigilante appeared out of nowhere, striking each of them with blows to the sternum and uppercuts to their chins, teeth flying in every direction. The guns went off, bullets whizzing through the summer air but missing their target. The men had no idea who or what was around them, feeling only intense pain with each invisible, powerful strike. The merciless assault continued. One by one they fell to the ground, writhing in pain and shrieking in agony. Wrists and ankles were broken, shoulders dislocated, noses shattered and relocated on the gang members' damaged faces. Pools of blood formed next to their thrashed bodies. The vigilante needed all of fifteen seconds to incapacitate his targets. All that remained was to finish off Esplanade and Blacksmith.

"Time to make your bones, Nicky." Esplanade pushed the young man forward into the moonlight, a jittery Blackstone whirling and pointing his gun toward the blackness of the night. Esplanade watched from a distance as his partner suddenly vanished without a sound.

"Nicky?" Esplanade called out. "Nicky, you ok?"

"Nicky's gone. Now it's your turn, Johnny."

Esplanade laughed. "I don't think so, mystery man."

On cue, powerful bright lights lit up the alley. Ten of Bianchi's men appeared on adjacent rooftops with spotlights and assault rifles. The vigilante stood still, illuminated and vulnerable, the man in black exposed for the first time. A woman appeared above, looking down from the rooftop of the six-story building, eyeing her ambushed adversary.

"Kill him!" Erica ordered. "Make sure there is nothing left of him!"

The night exploded with rapid gunfire, a hailstorm of bullets raining down into the alley. The vigilante dove to his left as the hot lead passed by his body. He hit the ground and kept moving as bullets slammed into the brick and asphalt around him. He had to stay in motion, one of the many skills Ernest had taught him high above Mount Tabor. He rolled and sprinted in different directions, moving like a snake avoiding a predator. Making his way up the alley, he bolted toward the street, the gunfire following him relentlessly until he made it on to Buckner Avenue. He outran the onslaught and the beams of light following him, blending with the night and disappearing after crossing West 34th Street.

"Where the hell did he go?" asked one voice from above.

"The subway!" shouted another. "Let's get down to the tracks!"

Esplanade looked up at his boss, hopeful his cohorts would find a body. "We did hit him, right?"

"I hope so," Erica sneered. "For all of your sake."

Esplanade hoped too. He knew what the penalty for failure was in the Bianchi organization. As Erica and her troops shut their lights and slid away, Esplanade ran back to where his Dodge was parked on West 33rd Street and jumped inside as police sirens wailed in the distance. "If this bastard's still alive," he said to himself. "I'm as good as dead."

He looked into his rear-view mirror to check for flashing lights, his heart stopping as he saw two flaming red eyes looking back at him.

"I've got bad news for you, Johnny."

Linda Esperanza was having coffee and gossiping with several other cops near the Western District stationhouse desk when the call came over the radio.

"10-10 shots fired. Numerous calls. West three-three and Buckner."

Esperanza tossed her coffee into the nearby garbage can and raced out the door, followed by several of her colleagues. She jumped into car number 2584 and tore off, lights and sirens, the location just six blocks from the stationhouse. She tried to see through the hazy fog that had settled, some movement ahead as she closed in. From a block away she could see a car, and a figure standing on the front hood, shrouded in smoke and moonlight as if it were posing for the arriving officers. The image was surreal.

"Oh God, its him!"

The police cruiser screeched to a halt, Linda quickly stepping out and taking cover behind the driver's side door. She unholstered her firearm and punched it out eye level, pointing it straight at the man in black atop the Dodge.

"Police, don't move!" she shouted, hoping her voice command didn't reek of the fear she was experiencing. "Let me see your hands!"

The vigilante complied and slowly raised his hands above his head as two other cruisers arrived on the scene, four more cops drawing their weapons and taking cover. He stood motionless as the officers shouted for him to get off the vehicle and down on the ground. He ignored the command as an ascending roar could be heard from a distance, above the cop's shouts.

"What the hell is that?" Linda asked herself, as the puzzled cops looked around the area. A dark, speeding vehicle tore up 34th Street, swung a wild turn onto Buckner and came to a smoldering and sudden stop where the vigilante stood. He jumped into the Bugatti Chiron and looked over at the driver.

"Let's get the hell out of here, Ernest."

"My thoughts exactly." said the driver.

The two-million-dollar sports car spun its wheels and exploded down Buckner, police bullets flying in its direction. The cops jumped back into their vehicles and began to pursue, a chase that lasted all of five seconds.

"In pursuit of a black sedan…holy shit," Linda said over her radio. "That car must be doing two hundred miles an hour!"

"Two fifty," another cop guessed as the taillights disappeared in the distance. "Say goodbye. He's gone."

Inside the hurtling sports car the vigilante slid down in the passenger seat, his heart pounding and adrenaline still running through him. He ran his hands along his body, searching for bullet wounds. Finding himself whole, he closed his eyes and swayed along with the powerful, twisting automobile. "Hey, any chance I can drive for a little bit?"

"None," Ernest grunted.

19

"There's five thousand friggin' shell casings, a mobster in his car with his ugly-ass face bashed in, three Hispano gang members twisted like pretzels, and not one goddam person saw anything? No one had a damn cell phone? This is getting stupid now!"

Linda withstood Lieutenant Morgan's angry rant as he paced back and forth around the crime scene, as several detectives and uniformed cops were marking evidence. "Well, Lieutenant, the Hispanos, as you call them, aren't going to be doing much talking for a few days. When Johnny Esplanade wakes up, maybe he can tell you who bounced his head off the dashboard a few times."

"That idiot better give me something," Morgan said as they headed over to the idling ambulance, where two paramedics attended to the badly beaten man. "The fool still alive?"

"Yeah, but you can't interview him now, lieutenant," one of the paramedics replied. "He's in and out, keeps losing consciousness."

"Well boo-friggin' hoo," Morgan said as he climbed into the ambulance, pushing the paramedics aside and hovering over Esplanade's prone body. "Hey Skippy, you want to tell me what happened here tonight?"

Esplanade opened his eyes slowly and saw the gold shield around Morgan's neck. "He's…the devil"

"The devil, huh? Like one of those horns-on-the-head, pitchfork carrying, Happy Halloween devils?"

Esplanade closed his eyes and shook his head slowly. "He ain't no joke, cop. He ain't human."

Morgan looked over at Linda standing outside the ambulance, listening intently. Each wore a look of disbelief.

"It wasn't the devil that turned your face into a goddam meatloaf casserole, Skippy. Who was it?" Morgan asked.

"You can't stop him. We can't either."

"You really are useless to me, you know that?" Morgan growled.

"Lieutenant," the paramedic interrupted. "We have to get this guy to the hospital. Interviews over."

Morgan jumped out as the doors closed behind him and the ambulance pulled away. The lieutenant and cop looked at each other, knowing exactly what the other was thinking.

"McSorley's going to have a goddam algorithm." Morgan said.

"You mean an aneurism." Linda corrected him.

"Whatever," Morgan said as he watched crime scene investigators and arriving press taking photos of the bloody Dodge. "The devil. Not human. A car that flies like a rocket ship. What the hell is this, the friggin' Twilight Zone?"

"Beats the hell out of me, lieutenant. But I know what I saw, and this guy is scary as shit."

Morgan surveyed the scene, eyeballing the inoperable surveillance cameras in the area. "Goddam weak politicians did this. Hey, where's your partner? I need you two to head to the hospital and keep an eye on Johnny Rotten over there."

"Tommy?" Linda asked. "He hasn't been around, took some time off. Might be going to Florida or something."

Morgan looked at the cop and raised an eyebrow. "Oh, really?"

As the cops exchanged suspicious looks, an anguished cry filled the night. "Somebody help my baby!"

Morgan and Linda looked over and saw a woman about twenty yards away, her nightgown covered in blood. Several uniformed cops ran toward her, shouting into their radios for another ambulance to respond immediately. The woman collapsed and fell to the ground, clutching the lifeless body of a small child.

"My baby!" she screamed, her heartbreaking shouts of grief rattling the already disturbed summer air. "My baby's been shot!"

Morgan's heart sank. "Good God, no."

"We wake this morning to the news we all feared the most; the war between the vigilante, the mob and police has taken its first innocent life. Five-year-old Shannon Moore, lying peacefully in her bed, hit by a stray bullet intended for the still unknown vigilante. This is why I got myself into this, to help try and avoid the inevitable. But I have failed, the police have failed, and organized crime pulled the fateful trigger. We are all complicit. The blood of little Shannon Moore is on the hands of all of us, including our esteemed Mayor, whose cowardice opened the floodgates which has led us to this day. I can no longer be a part of this. I have done nothing

of what I intended, and am responsible for the most devastating loss of life this heartless city has ever felt. Signing off for the final time. God Bless you little Shannon. I am truly sorry.

"God, forgive me."

-BlueWave.com

20

Winston and Ernest stood as the man dragged his tired body into the penthouse office on a scorching morning, temperatures reaching one hundred and three as the sun blazed through the large glass windows high above the city. He read the men's expressions, convinced they were already anticipating this moment and well prepared for it.

"I'm done," he said, tossing his black mask onto the desk. "But you already knew that."

Winston smiled and placed his hands on the man's slumped shoulders. "We are entering the final phase of our mission."

The man shook his head. "No, no more phases, no more mission. Moran's death was one thing, but now a little girl is dead because of me, because of us. I'm done, I'm out. No more."

"I feel your grief. It is not foreign to me, as you know. However, there is just one more thing for you to do," Winston said as he walked over to the sixty-four-inch television screen on the wall. "Did you happen to see the mayor's address this morning?" He turned on the television, and Mayor McSorley appeared on the screen.

"This morning, I spent time with the parents of Shannon Moore, the beautiful little girl who was struck by an errant bullet in the early morning hours," McSorley began. "I can't tell you how heartbreaking it was to hear these wonderful parents talk about their daughter, who was filled with life and love, only to be cut down by senseless violence. Violence caused by one person, and one person alone. The man who has been terrorizing our city, who believes he is above the law, and has brought back such painful memories of the pandemic by proclaiming himself to be a Black Plague. I cannot stand by and wait for the police to apprehend this person, as every day there are more and more Shannon Moore's being placed at risk while this man's evil actions continue. When my wife and I were accosted at the Murray Museum several nights ago, this coward asked me for my surrender. If indeed that's what it takes to stop this madness, then so be it. Tomorrow I will resign my position as Mayor of this great city and abdicate all power and jurisdiction over Harbor City, if one condition is met. This person must surrender to authorities, in my office, before six p.m. If he does, I will step down quietly so this city can move forward and away from these past few weeks of tragedy and fear."

The vigilante stood stunned. "He'll resign if I turn myself in?"

"That's what the mayor said," Winston answered. "Impotent and defeated, as was our plan."

"So, I go to prison?" the vigilante asked rhetorically. "That was the last phase of your plan all along?"

"No, of course not," Winston laughed. "You will go there tomorrow, surrender to the police only after the mayor formally resigns. The rest is up to you."

"Meaning?"

"Please, must I be so blunt? You surely can't be stopped by a few police officers, can you?"

He began running the scenario through his mind, and it seemed unfathomable. How could he outthink, overpower and escape what would undoubtedly be a small army of cops with an entire city watching? An insurmountable task, a ludicrous and ill-conceived plan. "It can't work, it won't work. I'm responsible for her death. I'll turn myself in, but I won't resist or escape."

Winston sighed loudly, exasperated. "Our goal was to force the removal of this Mayor, so Harbor City could rise again. Gone will be the weak appeasement policies of this administration. We will enter a time when a new leader emerges, brings law and order back to our streets, so we can live and prosper as once before. We are on the precipice of achieving such. We are about to make history, together."

The Black Plague had stopped listening.

###

Lieutenant Morgan banged his fist on the front door of 758 Esposito Drive, a modest one family home in the primarily middle-class Morrisville section of the city. The Ford F-150 that normally sat in the driveway was gone, while all the shades were drawn and air conditioning units silent. Still, Morgan was convinced the owner was home, and he wasn't about to leave without having a word or two with him.

Morgan looked around to make sure no one was watching before he slammed his foot against the door. It didn't budge. He tried again, with the same result. Frustrated, Morgan lifted his leg to try again, however this time the door swung open, causing the lunging, off-balance lieutenant to tumble face first onto the living room carpet. He felt the cold steel on the side of his face, the .357 Magnum pressed into his cheek.

"What the hell do you think you're doing?" Tommy Wilson asked angrily, cocking the hammer of the powerful revolver. "Breaking into my house? I could've killed you."

Lying on the floor, Morgan saw two large suitcases to the right of the door. "Just came by to wish you Bon Voyage, Wilson. Mind if I get up now?"

The hulking cop took a step back and stuffed the revolver into his waistband. "What the hell do you want, lieutenant?"

Morgan stood and straightened his tie. "I want to know where you were last night, and why the sudden urge to go traveling?"

"Is this an official department inquiry?" Wilson scowled. "If it is, I want my union attorney present. Otherwise, get your ass out of my house. I'm off-duty."

"A little girl died last night, because someone decided to take the law into their own hands and start a war. I'm gonna find that guy, and I'm gonna personally put the cuffs on him."

"I heard about the kid," Wilson said quietly, dropping his guard for a moment. "Damn shame."

"Is that why you're all packed up and running away? This whole scheme of yours just blew up in your face, huh Wilson?"

Wilson held back his anger. "This is what that drunk Lincoln is feeding you, right? I'm gonna tell you the same thing I told him. You think I'm the vigilante, then prove it."

Morgan smiled. "If I were you I'd cancel that vacation. Stick around the city for a while. Don't make me come looking for you again when it's time."

"You can't stop me, Lieutenant," Wilson said. "I have rights."

"So did that little girl," Morgan said as he left the house. "See ya soon, Skip."

21

St. Athanasius Church was filled and prepared for a funeral service befitting a Head of State. A small, mahogany casket, paid for by Charles Winston, lie in front of the altar, a sight so horrifically sad several arriving attendees fainted upon first glimpse. The first several pews were filled with city and state dignitaries, including Mayor McSorley, Governor Detwiler, and Police Commissioner Belanger in front. Seated next to Harbor City's top cop was Imani and Darnell Moore, Shannon's devastated parents.

Behind the family sat Winston and Ernest, alongside District Attorney Flagg and Chicago Mayor Ralph Paone. They spoke in hushed tones, commiserating over the dreadful loss of one so young and innocent. Lieutenant Morgan stood in the rear of the church, his eyes shifting as he looked over the crowd, convinced the vigilante was among them. Twenty-five police officers were posted outside and inside, at his command and ready for any attempts to disrupt the service.

Monsignor Joseph Altobelli entered the house of worship as the organ blared, the attendees rising to their feet in unison. He leaned over and kissed the casket before taking his place at the altar. He looked toward the Moore family, Imani crying uncontrollably in her husband's arms.

"There are no words to describe the pain of a parent losing a child, especially to such senseless and needless violence," the seventy-five-year-old pastor said, choking back his own emotions. "Our city has been through trying times the last two years. Our faith has been tested, but never like this. Never have we come face to face with Satan as we have now, but make no mistake, he is here, mocking our beliefs and taking away our most innocent."

Morgan fidgeted, the Pastor's words cutting through the cop's hardened skin. He looked over to his right and saw Lincoln standing in the corner, his head hung, and shoulders slumped. He started to make his way over to where his friend stood but decided against it, leaving his friend to mourn alone.

"When someone decides they are above God and man's laws, they take the dreaded step into Satan's lair, and all that can emanate from there is total darkness, the darkness that engulfs our city today." the Monsignor continued. "One of our brightest lights, young Shannon Moore, has been extinguished. The heart of our city has been wounded and is bleeding."

Overcome, Lincoln turned and headed for the church doors, hurrying past ushers inside, and a throng of media and residents gathered outside. Morgan watched his hasty exit before turning back to the crowd inside, looking for anything or anyone who seemed out of place.

"But our heart still beats," said the Monsignor, raising his hands to the Heavens. "Our heart still beats because Shannon has shone a light on the evil that we have ignored for far too long. Shannon did not die in vain. She is serving God and Jesus Christ by showing our elected officials and public servants that the time for looking the other way is over. It is a time for action, not words. Press conferences and fancy campaign slogans will not prevent another tragedy like Shannon Moore; bold action will. Jesus knew that, and it is time our so-called leaders realize it as well."

"Amen, Father," Morgan whispered. "A-friggin'-men."

McSorley felt every head inside the church turn in his direction, the heat of hundreds of eyes upon him causing him to bury his chin in his chest as the Monsignor's biting words continued.

"This Black Plague we have been hearing about has not been sent by God. It was not developed in a laboratory, and it is not the same as the virus that changed our lives forever. It is the Devil's work, Satan himself, and thus far the only soul that has stood before him with courage and bravery was this little, innocent child, betrayed by those who swore to protect her."

"Goddam right, Father," Morgan again whispered, before catching himself and looking up. "Oh, sorry. Bad habit."

"Shannon Moore," the Monsignor said, his voice finally cracking. "Please, save us all."

Keith Lincoln sat alone on the promenade bench looking out toward the Harbor Lighthouse, the early afternoon sun forcing him to squint as he watched the rolling waves crash into the rocks below. His mind was miles away, his ex-wife and young Shannon Moore occupying his thoughts. The pain and regret tore at him, his failure to stand up to City Hall after his political assassination at the hands of McSorley and Flagg ate away at his insides. He turned his back on his wife and used his firing as an excuse. Now, just as he was trying to absolve himself of responsibility in Mickey Moran's murder, another loss churned inside of him.

"Knew I'd find you here," Morgan said as he took a seat on the bench, shielding his eyes from the glare. "You always come here to think or sober up."

Lincoln managed a half-hearted smile, barely acknowledging the cop's arrival. He focused on the grey and blue pigeon nibbling at the grass to his left and admired the fact that the bird seemingly would never have to go through what he was feeling.

"Tommy Wilson is leaving town," Morgan said as a gust of warm air blew in from the water. "Taking vacation leave. I have nothing to hold him on, other than your suspicions, which holds about as much water as the friggin' Mohawk Desert."

"You mean Mojave."

"That's what I said," Morgan snapped. "Goddam it, Moran was ready to tell me who the ninja was. I'm sure he knew it was Wilson, and it was on his friggin' tongue before somebody blew his brains out and made sure he didn't talk. Could have been Erica, maybe the Amonte's, or Wilson himself. A lot of suspects."

"Maybe it won't matter after all. Maybe you'll get lucky and he'll surrender to McSorley tonight."

Morgan laughed. "You really think this guy's just gonna walk into City Hall and say here I am, arrest me? McSorley's an asshole, but he's not dumb. It's a public relations ploy, that's all it is. He looks like a hero. Look at me, willing to give up my political career to stop this menace and save the city. He knows damn well this dude ain't giving up anytime soon."

"I'm sorry, boss. I tried every connection I had, but no one knows anything, or they're just too scared to tell me."

"You blame them? Look at what just happened. They turned the streets into a war zone, a damn child takes a bullet, Moran gets whacked, and no one's doing a damn thing about it but hoping the dude surrenders. Flagg won't let us move on Bianchi because he has no spine, even though she's just as guilty as the damn ninja. No one trusts anyone. It's a goddam nightmare."

Lincoln nodded and sighed.

"You blame other people for not wanting to play this game anymore?" Morgan asked. "The cops are gonna lose faith again, and we're gonna totally lose the city. There's a part of me that wanted the ninja to win, enjoyed him kicking the shit out of these creepy bastards, but after the kid got shot…"

"There's no winners here, boss" Lincoln said, the defeat in his voice evident. "Only those left behind."

Morgan looked strangely at the man. "Deep, very deep. No idea what that means, though. Anyway, I gotta run. I gotta be in the Mayor's office just in case the ninja shows up. What a goddam joke. Go take a shower, Lincoln. You smell like piss and eggs."

Lincoln again tried to muster a smile or a laugh, but his clouded mind wouldn't respond. He continued listening to the crashing waves as he watched several pigeons congregate around his bench, pecking at the ground with not a care in the world. He looked up at the lighthouse and then out into the distance, wondering if there was any place in the world he could hide from his past and his present.

22

City Hall sat quietly as 6 p.m. approached, sealed off from the throngs of media held back two blocks in each direction by the police. Mayor McSorley ordered the building to be as accessible as possible in case the vigilante had accepted his invitation to surrender. Police Officers positioned themselves covertly throughout the four-story building, hidden in offices and restrooms to stay out of sight. The mayor sat behind his desk, Police Commissioner Belanger and Lieutenant Morgan at each side.

"Your people are ready, correct?" McSorley asked Belanger.

"We have spotters everywhere," she replied. "We created a safe passage for him if he comes peacefully. If not, our tactical team inside is in position, and we have snipers across the street locked onto this office."

"They can see us?" McSorley asked, looking around at the three office windows.

"There's one positioned on the rooftop directly behind you sir," the commissioner informed him. "No need to turn around. He's there."

McSorley, unnerved by the thought of high-powered rifles being pointed in his direction, started to panic. "Maybe this was a bad idea after all. We should call it off."

"Come on, your highness," Morgan said, shaking his head in disbelief. "You never really believed this dude was gonna show, did you?"

"I wouldn't have offered the deal if I didn't!" McSorley answered angrily. "Do you think this is some sort of stunt, lieutenant?"

"Sure smells like one, your eminence."

"Lieutenant, that's enough." Belanger snapped.

"Commissioner, when this is over, I want Lieutenant Morgan assigned to the abandoned auto lot on Cartwright Hill until the last minute of his fading career! Let him spend the rest of his nights talking to stray dogs and prostitutes!"

"Understood, sir." Belanger nodded.

Morgan ignored the mayor's bluster and the commissioner's appeasement, checking his watch repeatedly over the next several minutes. The three remained silent for nearly a half-hour. At 6:30, McSorley stood up.

"That's it. That's a wrap. He's not coming, and I'm not sitting around waiting for this coward. Commissioner, let's do a press conference-"

"City Hall Post 13! There's someone on the roof!"

Morgan's radio squealed as one of the snipers spotted a figure high atop the building. "Post 13, what's the description and exact location?"

"Northwest corner of the building…wearing all black…wait, I lost him…there he is, southeast side…he's gone!"

McSorley sat back down and fidgeted nervously in his chair as Belanger peered out the office's rear window.

"City Hall Post Seven! I need assistance…"

"Where's Post Seven?" the mayor asked, his teeth chattering as his nervous system went into a spasm.

"South East corner," Morgan said.

"He's headed down the South stairwell, coming right at us!"

"Do not stop him!" Morgan shouted into his radio. "Keep him in sight, but I repeat, do not engage-"

"Bullshit!" McSorley howled. "Shoot the bastard!"

"Wait. What?" Morgan asked.

Belanger seemed equally stunned. "Your honor, you yourself said-"

"I'm changing the plan!" McSorley hollered. "That lunatic doesn't enter this office!"

"This was not what you told the public!" Morgan yelled back. "You'll look like a fool-ass liar if they put this dude down."

"10-13! We need back-up! Third Floor! Get everybody up here!"

"He's coming for me," McSorley whined as he slid under his desk for cover. "He's coming for me. Do something!"

Morgan looked to Belanger, who shrugged her shoulders and spoke into her radio. "All units, you are authorized to use deadly physical force-"

"Shots fired, shots fired! Second floor landing!"

The sound of gunshots and shattered glass echoed down the hallway, reverberating through the mayor's office. McSorley crouched under his desk in a fetal position, his body trembling as Morgan and Belanger drew their service weapons.

"What's his goddam location?" Morgan asked. There was a sudden and eerie silence over the radio and inside the building. "City Hall units, what is the subject's location?"

The double doors swung open into the office, crashing into the walls behind them. An ominous figure stood before them, cloaked in black with satanic-like red eyes glaring outward. Four unconscious cops lie on the hallway floor behind him. Morgan and Belanger pointed their firearms at the nightmarish suspect. He took several steps closer before raising his hands over his head.

"We have a deal," the suspect said in a hushed tone, which only added to the fear that was palpable in the air. "I'm turning myself in. No resistance. Where is the mayor?"

Morgan and Belanger both turned their heads toward the desk and looked downward. McSorley climbed out, his knees buckling under him. He fell backwards into his chair, his jaw dropping at the sight of the man who had accosted him and his wife at the museum.

"Sorry, I…I…dropped a…contact lens," the mayor stuttered. "Who…who are you?"

"I am the Black Plague," he said. "I'm holding up my end of the deal. Now, Mr. Mayor, it's your turn."

McSorley swallowed hard and cleared his throat. "Okay, fair enough. I'm a man of great integrity, and I made this city a promise. However, pardon me if I don't trust a man who dresses like you and who assaulted police officers along with my wife, so I'm going to tweak our little deal. I am a negotiator, after all. I will publicly resign once you are safely in lockup."

The vigilante hesitated for a moment. "Fair enough, provided you don't reveal my identity until then. Deal?"

McSorley pondered the counter proposal. "No, I'm afraid that's not gonna work for me. I'm going to personally rip that mask off your head in front of the media outside and expose you to the people once and for all. That's the deal. Take it or leave it."

The vigilante shook his head. "Then there is no deal. So now, instead, I'm going to disarm both of your cops and beat you within an inch of your life before I throw you out that window behind you."

Morgan and Belanger gripped their weapons tighter and took aim. McSorley looked back and forth at them, his face turning ghostly white. "Okay, okay," the panic-stricken Mayor relented. "You win. I don't want any violence in this office. Like I said, I'm a man of integrity and I keep my word."

The vigilante slowly lowered his hands and placed them behind his back. "There will be no more bloodshed because of me. I surrender to you now in memory of Shannon Moore. There will be no others like her due to my actions."

Morgan quickly stepped forward and handcuffed the masked man. "You have the right to remain silent. Anything you say-"

"I'm waving my Miranda rights, officer."

"Take this man to prison," McSorley ordered. "Throw him in the hole. May he never see the light of day again!"

Morgan nodded and led the vigilante out of the office, down the hall and into a private elevator as arriving paramedics worked on the fallen officers. He kept one hand on his firearm, though he knew it would be fruitless should the suspect truly want to escape.

"Tell me something, Skippy, between you and I. What in the hell?"

"Not sure what you mean." he replied as the elevator descended toward the parking garage level two stories beneath City Hall. "Can you be more specific?"

"Why start all this shit, turn the city, the cops and the mob upside down, just to give up like this? Was it all about the kid dying, because my cop senses are tingling and I'm thinking there's more to this."

"My mission was to make McSorley and the criminals he released pay for their sins and the damage they caused during the pandemic," the vigilante said. "Some did, many more haven't, but ultimately one innocent life was too steep a price to pay."

The elevator door opened, and Morgan and his prisoner headed down parking aisle B toward his unmarked Chevrolet Impala. As they arrived at the car, Morgan opened the rear passenger side door and motioned for the man to get in.

"Between us, and completely off the record, I was really hoping you'd take that gutless, spineless McSorley down with you. A lot of us were. Damn, I would've let you beat the shit out of him upstairs while I played trivia on my cell phone. But I gotta job to do."

"That's good to know, Lieutenant," a voice bellowed from within the garage. Both men were stunned to see McSorley emerge from the dim stairwell, Belanger close behind. "I'm glad that opportunity never arose, for either of us."

A perplexed Morgan looked at both, unsure of what why they had followed him. "You forget to tell me something?" He looked to his left and saw the curvaceous, powerful body in a skin-tight black dress walking briskly towards him. "Erica?"

"Always the detective," she said as she stepped closer and struck the surprised cop on the side of his head with a lightning-fast right hook that sent Morgan sprawling up against his car and down to the cold cement floor. "Always a failure."

The vigilante, handicapped by his shackles, scrambled out of the backseat, only to run into the muzzle of a double-barreled sawed-off shotgun in the hands of Franco.

"McSorley you bastard. You made a deal with the mob?" a dazed Morgan asked the mayor as he writhed in pain on the ground, his head and neck aching from the blow.

"I make a lot of deals," McSorley smiled. "I'm a negotiator, remember?"

Morgan looked up at Belanger. "Commissioner, not you too?"

"The justice system is broken, for now," Belanger said, shaking her head in disgust. "This man must pay for his sins. This is the only way it ends."

Erica stood before the vigilante, who was still being held at the wrong end of Franco's shotgun. "The unmasking awaits." She drove her right knee into the vigilante's midsection, doubling him over. She followed with an uppercut to his jaw which rendered him unconscious.

23

The scent of the heavy air was unmistakable, the sound of the crackling waves all too familiar. The vigilante opened his eyes as gusts of wind blew off Lake Michigan, the powerful light above him illuminating the great body of water below. He knew exactly where he was, and who was standing in front of him.

"It's time to put all of the cards on the table," Erica said, her hair blowing wildly in the wind. "This is going to be quite painful for you, in so many ways."

He struggled, hands bound behind him and secured to the rusty, flimsy iron railing surrounding the Harbor City Lighthouse's observation deck, one hundred fifty feet above the roaring lake. Erica and Franco stood several feet away from him, their bodies flickering in the circulating light from the unmanned lantern.

"I afforded you the ultimate sign of respect by not removing your mask until now," she said, proud of her charitable ways. "No reason the mayor or any of his sycophantic minions should know who you are, or our connection."

"We have no connection, Erica," the vigilante said. "We aren't remotely alike."

"Oh, you'd be very surprised how strong a connection we have. The Black Plague? Catchy, but quite unimaginative. Lazy, in fact."

He stayed silent, ignoring her words and trying to pull his wrists free of the shackles.

"You have been transfigured," she said, altering her voice to resemble that of an older man. "You are now no longer just a man. You are wrath. Those that destroyed my city, took my wife from me, will now feel the wrath of God, my wrath, far worse than the virus that began our fall. Retribution and rebirth."

A sickening feeling filled his body. He had heard those words before. He again tried to free himself, the cuffs too tight and the rickety guardrail offering little support. He tried to block the woman's voice from his head, to focus on an escape, but her taunts were angering him more and more.

"You know I was his first, and he obviously didn't tell you about me," she said with amusement. "That's right, I was Alfonse Bianchi's daughter, but I grew tired of being just that, of my father and his men fighting my battles for me. I trained night and day with the top martial artists my father's money could buy. I didn't want to grow up needing him or anyone else. Then one day, a driver pulls up, says his boss would like to meet me. He fills my head with all this talk about becoming the guardian of the city, about rejecting my father's evil ways and rising above it all to save Harbor City. He took me to Mount Tabor, the Church of the Transfiguration, and put me through hell until I was ready, even let me drive one of his million-dollar sports cars."

"He let you drive?" the vigilante asked with a sardonic smile, hiding the fire building inside him.

"He seduced me with power, branded me the Black Plague. Wicked, but I was going to have to be, to overcome those who would come after me, including my very own father."

"Then why did you turn into this?" he asked. "Why abandon his plan to save the city, just to become a common thug?"

"You are so naïve, but I can't condemn you for that. So was I. His plan to save Harbor City wasn't anything like that at all. It was never about the virus, criminals or even about his dearly departed wife."

"You're a liar!" he raged, lunging toward her but reined in by his restraints, tugging mercilessly at the guardrails. "You took what he gave you and you betrayed him!"

"You poor, ignorant man. He is the only liar. He wanted McSorley out of power, yes, but not because of what he told you and I. Before the pandemic hit, he had a real estate deal that was going to rival Chicago's skyline. No longer would Harbor City be dwarfed by our big brother. He

was going to change that, replace Chicago as the media capital of the Midwest, and he would be the ultimate power broker. But McSorley wouldn't play ball, rejected all the rezoning plans. The crime wave was a perfect excuse. Yes, you exposed the lie about McSorley's wife and her connections to Oliver Industries and the forced vaccinations, but you didn't realize the Big Lie was really about Anna."

"What about Anna?"

"Those four men you killed, in revenge for her murder. They were patsies, paid off to take the fall, assured the case would be thrown out because the District Attorney was going to set up the arresting officer and make it all go away. Flagg was playing both sides, paid off by the old man himself. Our friend Charles knew random crime wouldn't be enough to shock voters into ousting McSorley, but the city's most famous woman being murdered in broad daylight? Changed the game. So it was all about real estate, not his wife. Land before love. But you missed that too, didn't you?"

The vigilante seethed. "Why should I believe a word out of your mouth?"

"Because he had me kill Anna Winston!" she shouted. "I did it, and then I killed my father! He was weak, vulnerable. I took the power Charles gave me and took over this wretched city before my father lost it all."

The vigilante became silent and motionless, paralyzed by confusion as Franco walked over and tore off his mask.

"Well, apparently I am a fool as well," Erica lamented, surprised at the sight of Keith Lincoln. "The disgraced detective who came to me looking for a way out, I imagine. But I guess failure has been a big part of your life, correct? You failed to uncover the Winston murder plot, and you failed your wife a while ago, right? I do my homework, detective."

"You know nothing about me." he snarled.

"I know you also failed to bring down McSorley, and worst of all, you failed that poor, innocent girl, caught in the crossfire you created. Such a shame to lose a little one like that. So young, so very young and pure. I was like that once, till my father and Charles Winston poisoned my soul forever. That's why I had to kill my father, and why I will kill Charles Winston after I've killed you."

In a rage, the vigilante summoned all his strength, thrusting his body forward. The guardrail separated from the aged concrete walkway, the restraints sliding off as the metal twisted and snapped the cuffs in half. Franco raised his shotgun, but the vigilante was too fast. He slammed into Franco, pinning the man up against the lighthouse wall with a thud that drove the air from the man's lungs. He took the palm of his hand and slammed it into Franco's throat. The bodyguard made a gurgling sound before his body slithered lifelessly to the ground.

"Well done, Mr. Lincoln," Erica said, stepping over Franco's dead body. "But it was always going to come down to you and I."

The vigilante stepped forward and took a fighting stance. Erica followed suit, the two squaring off as a cold mist blew in off the lake below. Erica snapped off a quick left jab that he avoided easily. He threw a right cross that Erica blocked, the woman countering with a side kick to the outside of the man's knee. His leg buckled as Erica quickly followed with a thrust kick to his chest that sent the man sprawling backwards to the ledge of the platform.

"Even transfiguration could not save Jesus Christ from death," Erica said as she approached her fallen adversary. "Are you ready to die, Mr. Lincoln?"

He wailed in pain as the woman's right stiletto heel crashed into his left side, his ribs breaking with a sickening crackle sound. He covered up to fend off another kick, then slid his legs up to steady his feet underneath his prone body. With sudden force, he leaped up and grabbed Erica by the throat, driving her into the lighthouse wall and slamming the back of her head into the concrete. He drove her head into the wall again, placed the palm of his hand over her eyes and drove her one more time into the unforgiving concrete. Erica dropped to her knees, looked up at him, and fell unconscious.

"No, I'm not ready," he said, collapsing to his knees, his chest heaving as his broken ribs throbbed. After several minutes, he composed himself and found a way to ignore the intense pain, standing and looking back at the lights of the city he now cursed.

"All of it was a lie," he said to himself as fog rolled in from the lake. "Everything I've done and believed. That was the biggest lie of all."

A sharp, piercing pain suddenly shot up his back. He tumbled forward, gagging as blood ran from his mouth. Down on all fours, he looked over his shoulder and saw an unsteady Erica swaying in the wind with a jagged knife in her hand.

"You turned your back on a woman once before, right?" she taunted him. "You should have learned your lesson." Erica stalked him as he tried to crawl away, the vigilante rolling to the edge of the platform and looking down at the rocks and black water below. "Goodbye, Mr. Lincoln. Say hello to my father in hell."

A gunshot rang out and echoed across the lake. Erica fell, horrific pain in her left shoulder. She looked up and saw the man who arrested her father years ago holding the smoking gun.

"You're under arrest, you crazy, psycho bitch!" Morgan shouted. "I'm tired of your shit!"

The vigilante sat up, blood still running from his mouth. "What the hell took you so damn long?"

Morgan was stunned by the vision of Lincoln encased in black. "Skippy? On my Aunt Thelma's drunken soul, you've got to be freakin' kidding me?"

Erica grabbed the knife at her feet and in one motion violently hurled it toward Morgan's head, missing the cop by less than an inch. The vigilante rose and grabbed Erica by her hair, lifting her off the ground. She fought back, striking him on the left side of his jaw. The two grabbed onto each other, locked in a tight clench, as they struggled on the platform edge.

"This is our destiny," Erica said as the two exhausted every ounce of their strength while Morgan struggled to find a clear shot.

The vigilante shifted his body and placed his right arm under her left. He grabbed her right leg, crouched, and lifted her off the ground and over his head, utilizing every ounce of strength left in his beaten body. "No, it's yours!"

Erica's scream could be heard for miles, as her body tumbled down the side of the lighthouse, slamming into the rocks and sliding into Lake Michigan. He watched as the water rippled, her body disappearing into the massive deep. Morgan walked over and joined him at the edge.

"Adios, you goddam lunatic," Morgan said, relieved the woman was gone. He looked at the vigilante and still couldn't believe his eyes. "It was you all this time, Skippy? How is that possible? You barely wash your ass or change your socks."

"Boss," Lincoln whispered as he fell into Morgan's arms. "Shut up and get me to a hospital."

Morgan held onto the man, struggling to support his weight "Okay, I got you, pal." They trudged slowly toward the stairwell. "So tell me, Skippy, the wine and the women, it was all bullshit? Moran, Wilson, your stupid blob-"

"All of it," Lincoln said. "But it's not over. Charlie Winston has to be stopped. He's behind all of this."

"Charlie Winston?" Morgan asked, surprised by the revelation. "That wrinkled old bat?"

"He had his wife killed, boss. It was all a lie."

Morgan's head was spinning as they hit the top step and looked down. "Goddam stink bugs everywhere in this city!"

"Yes, there are." Ernest appeared at the landing below them, pulling a nine-millimeter from his waistband and firing three shots, each striking Lincoln in the chest. The vigilante jerked backwards and stumbled against the old, broken railing, the iron pulling away from its moorings and giving way. He fell off the deck, dropping from the sky into the lake, hitting the water with a sickening splash before vanishing in the darkness just feet from where Erica had disappeared.

"Noooo!" Morgan screamed as he ran to the edge and looked down. "What the hell did you just do, you dumb bastard?" He spun and scrambled back to the stairs, but Ernest was gone. He began sobbing, praying his friend would emerge from the rolling waves. He closed his eyes and tried to wake up from what he hoped was a bad dream, but the nightmare was real, as was the evil he had just encountered.

24

"We're awarding you the Medal of Honor tomorrow," Mayor McSorley said as he and Commissioner Belanger sat inside the City Hall office, going over Lieutenant Morgan's reports. "So, with that in mind, I'm recommending you rewrite some of these. There's information in there that might be too sensitive for the general public."

"Like what, exactly?" Morgan asked, his head and body still aching. "The part about you being in bed with the mob, or the part about Charlie Winston being a conspirator to murder?"

"Both of those, actually," McSorley said flippantly. "None of that is what this city needs right now. What they need is to hear about the hero cop who stopped the mafia boss and her accomplice, the Black Plague vigilante. We need to celebrate, not throw around baseless allegations that won't do anyone any good."

"You mean won't do your career any good," Morgan fired back. "I'm requesting a warrant for the arrest of Charlie Winston."

"Denied, lieutenant," Belanger replied sternly. "Erica Bianchi and Franco Toscano were killed in self-defense by yourself during police action. That is exactly what happened, and you will spell that out in your revised reports. Besides, you were almost killed yourself. Traumatized. Your memory is tainted. Your testimony, as presently spelled out, simply won't hold up."

"Charlie Winston needs to be arrested." Morgan insisted.

"On the word of a law breaking, murderous vigilante?" Belanger countered. "Where's your evidence, lieutenant? You weren't even able to identify who this Black Plague was."

"Charlie Winston's man-servant killed him before I could," Morgan said angrily. "I recognized the big goon immediately. He needs to be brought in and charged with murder, on my word!"

"Lieutenant, you need to see the bigger picture here," McSorley said. "You are going to be looked at as the modern-day Eliot Ness, the lawman that went to war with a vicious mob boss and won. Throw in the vigilante aspect and you're going to be the most famous cop in the country for a long time. You'll retire a legend."

"Who said I was retiring?" Morgan asked. "No, no way, not now. You think I'm walking away from this? Nah, you're stuck with me. I'm gonna bring a shitstorm down on both your heads. You just watch."

As Morgan stormed out and slammed the door behind him, the mayor and commissioner sat quietly for a moment, weighing their options.

"We can slander him, set him up as a dirty cop who aided the vigilante," Belanger mused. "Destroy every ounce of his credibility so no one will listen."

"We could," McSorley said as he pondered his next step. "Or we can wait and see who takes over the Bianchi organization, make a deal with them, and let them take care of it so our hands stay clean. Morgan isn't our only problem, though. Charlie Winston won't stop, and he knows we can't touch him. He'll send someone else after me, so if you want to keep your job, you'd better come up with a way to stop both."

Belanger nodded. "I'll take care of everything, your honor. What about Lincoln?"

"Him?" McSorley grunted. "With the vigilante gone he'll have nothing to write that anyone cares about. He'll go back to writing stories about ticket fixing and low police morale. He's irrelevant now, and no longer our concern."

Lieutenant Morgan grabbed a cab and headed downtown to his apartment, his mind exhausted and his thoughts jumbled. He kept replaying the events on the lighthouse in his mind, going over each step he took, wondering if there was anything he could have done differently to avert his friend's death. Angry at himself, he opened the front door to his home and trudged up the stairs to his second-floor bedroom, throwing his coat on the floor and collapsing on his bed.

He closed his eyes and saw his friend falling and falling, the image now burned into his consciousness. He questioned himself as to how he didn't realize Keith Lincoln, so close to him, was the vigilante he was hunting. How could he have allowed this to slip by him? How could Lincoln have filled his head with so many lies? Perhaps it was age, cynicism or just blind loyalty, but Morgan knew he had failed the biggest test of his career.

What next, he thought? The Mayor and Police Commissioner would stop at nothing to keep him silent and would undoubtedly try and force his retirement. The District Attorney's office was compromised already by the McSorley administration, so that wasn't an option. The media? Why would they take the words of a cop over those of a billionaire, a mayor and his top law enforcement official? There simply was no way out.

Morgan's mind slowed long enough for him to fall asleep, the prescription pain medication he had just ingested quickly taking effect. Several hours later he woke up, the pills he had swallowed fogging his mind. He splashed water on his face and started a pot of coffee, before sitting down in front of his computer to see what the local news was saying. As the screen lit up, it took him to the last page he visited, Bluewave.com. He started to close it out, before realizing there was a new post, placed on the site just two hours earlier. He tried to clear his head as he read along, cursing the drugs and the weak coffee he was drinking.

The water is cold, my death temporary…

Those responsible walk the streets as free men and women, mocking our laws and our justice system while pocketing fortunes built on blood, corruption and, of course, deadly disease. As we've learned, trusting your government, your leaders, your elected officials is a tragic mistake, as blind faith will guarantee you the same fate as the vigilante…for now.

The Black Plague will rise again.'

"Goddam, Skippy," Morgan groaned. "I figured you were too damn stupid to die."

THE END

ACKNOWLEDGMENTS

Cynthia, Layla and Talia- My three girls who make me proud each day. Daddy loves you.

Lia Rose- The newest addition to the family, who brings smiles to all our faces.

Joseph- My brother, and the most talented writer there is.

Kathy- My partner, who pushes me with her love and support.

Mom and Dad- They have always made everything seem possible.

ABOUT THE AUTHOR

Billy Pepitone is a retired member of the New York City Police Department, having served twenty years in the nation's largest local law enforcement agency. During his decorated career, the Brooklyn, New York native was a first responder to numerous high-profile incidents, including both World Trade Center attacks. Upon his retirement he co-wrote the critically acclaimed baseball/fantasy novel 'Soul of a Yankee' with his brother Joseph, and has published several other works in different genres, utilizing his law enforcement experiences to bring fresh, new characters and stories to life.

In 2020, Billy was an endorsed candidate for Mayor of New York City.

He currently resides in Staten Island, New York, with his three daughters.